John Hyde, William Crookes, C. Wood Davis

The Wheat Problem

based on remarks made in the presidential address to the British association at

Bristol in 1898, revised

John Hyde, William Crookes, C. Wood Davis

The Wheat Problem
based on remarks made in the presidential address to the British association at Bristol in 1898, revised

ISBN/EAN: 9783337396749

Printed in Europe, USA, Canada, Australia, Japan

Cover: Foto ©Andreas Hilbeck / pixelio.de

More available books at **www.hansebooks.com**

THE WHEAT PROBLEM

BASED ON REMARKS MADE IN THE PRESIDENTIAL
ADDRESS TO THE BRITISH ASSOCIATION
AT BRISTOL IN 1898

REVISED WITH AN ANSWER TO VARIOUS CRITICS

By SIR WILLIAM CROOKES, F.R.S.

WITH TWO CHAPTERS ON THE FUTURE WHEAT SUPPLY OF THE
UNITED STATES, BY MR C. WOOD DAVIS, OF PEOTONE, KANSAS,
AND THE IION. JOHN HYDE, CHIEF STATISTICIAN TO THE
DEPARTMENT OF AGRICULTURE, WASHINGTON

LONDON
JOHN MURRAY, ALBEMARLE STREET
1899

PREFACE

THE present volume arises out of the comments and criticisms provoked by the Address I delivered before the Members of the British Association in September 1898. There were difficulties in the presentation of my subject. Limited to little more than an hour, I was compelled, from consideration to my audience, to deal with the results of study rather than with details leading to such results. And constrained by respect for my responsible position to treat the matter soberly and without exaggeration, it was impossible for me to do more than barely to outline the serious peril awaiting wheat-eaters who contentedly pursue the present wasteful system of cultivation. My remarks took the form of a warning rather than of a prophecy. To put the matter briefly, I stated that under present conditions of heedless culture, a scarcity of wheat is within appreciable distance ; that wheat-growing land all over the world is becoming exhausted, and that at some future time—in my opinion not far distant—no available wheat land will be left. But I also pointed out that Nature's resources, properly utilised, are ample. I urged that, instead of being satisfied with an average world-yield of 12.7 bushels an acre, a moderate dressing of chemical manure would pull up the average to 20 bushels—thus postponing the day of dearth " to so distant a period that we and our sons and grandsons may legitimately live without undue solicitude for the future."

It was far from my intention to create a sensation, or to indulge in a " cosmic scare." After considerable study, I placed before the public hard and formidable *facts*. I have been assailed with criticism—unfavourable, abusive, suggestive—but, having pondered disputed points, I cannot in any material degree modify my estimates of the future producing capacity of the wheat fields of the globe.

In preparing this volume, I have endeavoured to give in greater fulness the data on which my conclusions are based. The actual and potential wheat-producing capacity of the United States is—and will be for years to come—the dominant factor in the world's bread supply. I therefore give prominence

to criticisms launched against me in refutation
of the intrinsic part of my argument. I have had
invaluable assistance from Mr Wood Davis of
Peotone, Kansas, a wheat grower and statistician of
recognised authority. Mr Davis appears to be the
sole person who deals with the problem in a manner
to determine such essential factors as average acre
yields for long periods, unit requirements for each of
the primary food staples of the temperate zones, and
the ratios existing during different recent periods
between the consuming populations and the acres
employed in the production of each of the primary
food staples. Mr Davis has contributed to this
volume a chapter in which he goes over the whole
ground, and practically corroborates all my statements.

I am also permitted to include in my volume, by
the kindness of the proprietors of the *North American Review*, an article written by the Honble. John
Hyde, Chief Statistician to the Agricultural Department of the United States, in which the wheat
problem is discussed with especial reference to the
future food supply of the States. In an appendix
I include still later figures received from Mr
Hyde.

I have no wish to be gloomy, and certainly no wish to consider myself infallible. If at the end of another generation of wasteful culture my forecast is invalidated by the *Unforeseen*, I cheerfully invite friends and critics to stone me as a false prophet.

WILLIAM CROOKES.

July 1899.

CONTENTS

THE WHEAT PROBLEM *

I

STATEMENT OF THE PROBLEM

FOR the third time in its history the British Association meets in your City of Bristol. The first meeting was held under the presidency of the Marquis of Lansdowne in 1836, the second under the presidency of Sir John Hawkshaw in 1875. Formerly the President unrolled to the meeting a panorama of the year's progress in physical and biological sciences. To-day, the President usually restricts himself to specialities connected with his own work, or deals with questions which, for the time, are uppermost. To be President of the

---

* This forms the major portion of my Presidential Address, delivered before the British Association for the Advancement of Science, at Bristol, on the evening of 7th September 1898. The only alterations I have made are the corrections of one or two minor inaccuracies, and the incorporation of the matter originally consigned to an Appendix into the body of the Address.

British Association is undoubtedly a great honour.
It is also a great opportunity and a great
responsibility; for I know that, on the wings
of the Press, my words, be they worthy or not,
will be carried to all points of the compass. I
propose to deal with the important question of
the supply of bread to the inhabitants of these
Islands. I shall not attempt any general survey
of the sciences; these, so far as the progress in
them demands attention, will be more fitly brought
before you in the different Sections, either in the
Addresses of the Presidents or in communications
from Members.

And now I owe a sort of apology to this
brilliant audience. I must ask you to bear with
me for ten minutes, for I am afraid what I now
have to say will prove somewhat dull. I ought to
propitiate you, for, to tell the truth, I am bound to
bore you with figures. Statistics are rarely attrac-
tive to a listening audience; but they are necessary
evils, and those of this evening are unusually dole-
ful. Nevertheless, when we have proceeded a little
way on our journey I hope you will see that the
river of figures is not hopelessly dreary. The
stream leads into an almost unexplored region, and
to the right and left we see channels opening out,
all worthy of exploration, and promising a rich

reward to the statistic explorer who will trace them to their source—a harvest—as Huxley expresses it, "immediately convertible into those things which the most sordidly practical of men will admit to have value, namely, money and life." My chief subject is of interest to the whole world—to every race—to every human being. It is of urgent importance to-day, and it is a life and death question for generations to come. I mean the question of Food supply. Many of my statements you may think are of the alarmist order; certainly they are depressing, but they are founded on stubborn facts. They show that England and all civilised nations stand in deadly peril of not having enough to eat. As mouths multiply, food resources dwindle. Land is a limited quantity, and the land that will grow wheat is absolutely dependent on difficult and capricious natural phenomena. I am constrained to show that our wheat-producing soil is totally unequal to the strain put upon it. After wearying you with a survey of the universal dearth to be expected, I hope to point a way out of the colossal dilemma. It is the chemist who must come to the rescue of the threatened communities. It is through the laboratory that starvation may ultimately be turned into plenty.

The food supply of the kingdom is of peculiar

interest to this meeting, considering that the grain trade has always been, and still is, an important feature in the imports of Bristol. The imports of grain to this city amount to about 25,000,000 bushels per annum—8,000,000 of which consist of wheat.

What are our home requirements in the way of wheat? The consumption of wheat per head of the population (unit consumption) is over 6 bushels per annum; and taking the population at 40,000,000, we require no less than 240,000,000 bushels of wheat, increasing annually by 2,000,000 bushels, to supply the increase of population. Of the total amount of wheat consumed in the United Kingdom we grow 25 and import 75 per cent.

So important is the question of wheat supply that it has attracted the attention of Parliament, and the question of national granaries has been mooted. It is certain that, in case of war with any of the great Powers, wheat would be contraband, as if it were cannon or powder, liable to capture even under a neutral flag. We must therefore accept the situation, and treat wheat as munitions of war, and grow, accumulate, or store it as such. It has been shown that at the best our stock of wheat and flour amounts only to 64,000,000 bushels—fourteen weeks' supply—while last April our stock was equal to only 10,000,000 bushels, the smallest ever recorded by *Beerbohm* for the period of the season. Similarly, the stocks held in Europe, the United States, and Canada, called "the world's visible supply," amounted to only 54,000,000 bushels, or 10,000,000 less than last year's sum total, and nearly 82,000,000 less than that of 1893 or 1894 at the corresponding period. To arrest this impending danger, it has been proposed that an amount of 64,000,000 bushels of wheat should be purchased by the State, and stored in national granaries, not to be opened except to remedy deterioration of grain, or in view of national disaster rendering starvation imminent. This 64,000,000 bushels would add another fourteen weeks' life to the population; assuming that the ordinary stock had not been drawn on, the wheat in the country would only then be enough to feed the population for twenty-eight weeks.

I do not venture to speak authoritatively on national granaries. The subject has been discussed in the daily Press, and the recently published Report from the Agricultural Committee on National Wheat Stores brings together all the arguments in favour of this important scheme, together with the difficulties to be faced if it be carried out with necessary completeness.

More hopeful, although difficult and costly, would be the alternative of growing most, if not all our own wheat supply here at home in the British Isles. The average yield over the United Kingdom last year was 29.07 bushels per acre, the average for the last eleven years being 29.46. For twelve months we need 240,000,000 bushels of wheat, requiring about 8,250,000 acres of good, wheat-growing land, or nearly 13,000 square miles, increasing at the rate of 100 square miles per annum, to render us self-supporting as to bread food. This area is about one-fourth the size of England.

Last year there were under corn crops in the United Kingdom :—

Wheat .	.	3,025 sq. miles, producing 56,296,000 bushels.
Barley .	.	3,447 ,,
Oats .	.	6,580 ,,
TOTAL .	13,052	,,

There is now as much area under mixed cereals as would have to be devoted solely to wheat to make our country self-supporting.

A total area of land in the United Kingdom

equal to a plot 110 miles square, of quality and climate sufficient to grow wheat to the extent of 29 bushels per acre, does not seem a hopeless demand.*   It is doubtful, however, if this amount of land could be kept under wheat, and the necessary expense of high farming faced, except under the imperious pressure of impending starvation, or the stimulus of a national subsidy or permanent high prices.   Certainly these 13,000 square miles would not be available under ordinary economic conditions, for much, perhaps all, the land now under barley and oats would not be suitable for wheat.   In any case, owing to our cold, damp climate and capricious weather, the wheat crop is hazardous, and for the present our annual deficit of 180,000,000 bushels must be imported.   A permanently higher price for wheat is, I fear, a calamity that ere long must be faced.   At enhanced prices, land now under wheat will be better farmed, and therefore will yield better, thus giving increased production without increased area.

The burning question of to-day is, What can the United Kingdom do to be reasonably safe from starvation in presence of two successive failures of the world's wheat harvest, or against a hostile com-

---

* The total area of the United Kingdom is 120,979 square miles ; therefore the required land is about a tenth part of the total.

bination of European nations? We eagerly spend
millions to protect our coasts and commerce; and
millions more on ships, explosives, guns, and men;
but we omit to take necessary precautions to supply
ourselves with the very first and supremely important munition of war—food.

To take up the question of food-supply in its
scientific aspect, I must not confine myself exclusively to our own national requirements. The
problem is not restricted to the British Isles—the
bread-eaters of the whole world share the perilous
prospect—and I do not think it out of place if, on
this occasion, I ask you to take with me a wide,
general survey of the wheat supply of the whole
world.

Wheat is the most sustaining food grain
of the great Caucasian race which includes the
peoples of Europe, United States, British
America, the white inhabitants of South Africa,
Australasia, parts of South America, and the
white population of the European colonies. Of
late years the individual consumption of wheat
has almost universally increased. In Scandinavia
it has risen 100 per cent. in twenty-five years;
in Austro-Hungary, 80 per cent.; in France, 20
per cent.; while in Belgium it has increased 50
per cent. Only in Russia and Italy, and possibly

Turkey, has the consumption of wheat per head declined.

In 1871 the bread-eaters of the world numbered 371,000,000. In 1881 the numbers rose to 416,000,000; in 1891, to 472,600,000, and at the present time they number 516,500,000. The augmentation of the world's bread-eating population in a geometrical ratio is evidenced by the fact that the yearly aggregates grow progressively larger. In the early seventies they rose 4,300,000 per annum, while in the eighties they increased by more than 6,000,000 per annum, necessitating annual additions to the bread supply nearly one-half greater than sufficed twenty-five years ago.

How much wheat will be required to supply all these hungry mouths with bread? At the present moment it is not possible to get accurate estimates of this year's wheat crops of the world, but an adequate idea may be gained from the realised crops of some countries and the promise of others. To supply 516,500,000 bread-eaters, if each bread-eating unit is to have his usual ration, will require a total of 2,324,000,000 bushels for seed and food. What are our prospects of obtaining this amount?

According to the best authorities, the total supplies from the 1897-98 harvest are 1,921,000,000 bushels.*   The requirement of the 516,500,000

TABLE I.

* The World's Wheat Crop of 1897-98 from Contributory Areas. [1]

	BUSHELS		BUSHELS
United States . .	510,000,000	Uruguay, Brazil, etc. .	9,000,000
France . . .	240,000,000	Portugal . . .	7,000,000
Russia and Poland .	230,000,000	Servia . . .	6,000,000
Austria-Hungary .	135,000,000	Holland . . .	5,000,000
Germany . . .	105,000,000	Denmark . . .	5,000,000
Spain. . . .	96,000,000	Sweden and Norway .	5,000,000
Italy	82,000,000	Greece . . .	4,000,000
Trans-Caucasia and Siberia	64,000,000	Switzerland . .	4,000,000
Argentina . . .	60,000,000	Bosnia, Montenegro, Cy-	
United Kingdom .	56,000,000	prus, etc. . .	4,000,000
Canada . . .	55,000,000	South Africa . .	4,000,000
Roumania . . .	43,000,000		
Caucasia (Northern) .	40,000,000		1,890,000,000
Australasia . . .	38,000,000	Add imports from Asia	
Bulgaria . . .	30,000,000	and North Africa .	31,000,000
Turkey in Europe .	22,000,000		
Belgium . . .	16,000,000	Total available wheat	
Chili	15,000,000	supply . . .	1,921,000,000

TABLE II.

Table showing the Variations in the Bread-eating Populations, and the Available Supply of Wheat in the Five Yearly Periods from 1878 to 1897, in Millions of Bushels, and Annual Averages.

YEARS	Bread-eating Populations	Wheat grown by 'Contributory areas'	Imports from Asia and North Africa	Remainders from former harvest	Total available supply	Required for seed and food	Supply in excess of year's needs
1877-81	407.0	1797.0	13.8	174.4	1985.2	1812.8	172.4
1882-86	432.8	1937.6	41.4	294.0	2273.0	1946.0	327.0
1887-91	460.8	2043.5	43.2	260.2	2346.9	2102.0	244.9
1892-96	490.9	2199.2	23.6	265.4	2488.2	2233.8	254.4
1897-98	510.0	1890.0	31.0	300.0	2221.0	2310.0	Deficit 89.0

[1] Outside the better known areas of wheat supply a certain proportion of wheat comes from India, Persia, Syria, Anatolia, and North Africa. But it is impossible to get accurate figures as to acreage and yield from these countries; as bread-eaters derive less than one per cent. of their supplies from these out-lying sources, it is convenient to call the ordinary areas "contributory areas," and to deal with the external areas no further than to show the volume of imports yielded from year to year.

bread-eaters for seed and food are 2,324,000,000 bushels; there is thus a deficit of 403,000,000 bushels, which has not been urgently apparent owing to a surplus of 300,000,000 bushels carried over from the last harvest. Respecting the prospects of the harvest year just beginning, it must be borne in mind that there are no remainders to bring over from last harvest. We start with a deficit of 103,000,000 bushels, and have 6,500,000 more mouths to feed. It follows, therefore, that one-sixth of the required bread will be lacking unless larger drafts than now seem possible can be made upon early produce from the next harvest.

The import requirements for wheat are as follows :—

TABLE III.

	BUSHELS		BUSHELS
United Kingdom, about	180,000,000	Spain	10,000,000
Belgium . . .	24,000,000	Portugal . . .	4,000,000
Germany . . .	35,000,000	Greece	4,500,000
Holland . . .	13,000,000	Denmark . . .	2,000,000
Switzerland . . .	13,500,000	Islands and tropical lands	42,000,000
France	40,000,000		
Sweden . . .	4,000,000	TOTAL .	372,000,000

The majority of the wheat crops between 1882 and 1896 were in excess of current needs, and thus considerable reserves of wheat were available for supplementing small deficits from the four deficient harvests. But bread-eaters have almost eaten up the reserves of wheat, and the 1897 harvest being under average, the conditions become serious.

Between 1882 and 1897 the wheat crops were so abundant that over 1,200,000,000 bushels were added to our stores, beside large accumulations of rye. During this time of golden harvests, the exports from Russia increased, in consequence of the Russian decline in unit consumption of 13.5 per cent. These reserves have been gradually drawn upon, but enough still remained to obscure the fact that the 1895-96 harvest was 75,000,000 bushels, and the 1896-97 harvest was 138,000,000 bushels below current needs.

The following table has been compiled from statistics carefully collected by Mr Davis and other observers.* The prophetic figures are on the

* I have taken the unit consumption including seed at 4.5 bushels and the yield per acre at 12.7 bushels per annum, this being the average of the whole world. The exact yield varies with the country in which wheat is grown, as shown by the following table :—

TABLE IV.

Average Yield of Wheat per Acre in—

	BUSHELS		BUSHELS
Denmark	41.8	Poland	16.2
United Kingdom	29.1	Canada	15.5
New Zealand	25.5	Argentina	13.0
Norway	25.1	Italy	12.1
Germany	23.2	United States (mean)	12.0
Belgium	21.5	Australasia	10.0
Holland	21.5	India	9.2
France	19.4	Russia in Europe	8.6
Hungary	18.6	Algeria	7.5
Roumania	18.5	South Australia	7.0
Austria	16.3		

assumption that population, unit consumption, and steady development will increase during the next forty-three years as they have increased since 1871 :—

TABLE V.

Date	Bread-eaters	Food and Seed * required per unit. Bushels	Requiring bushels of wheat	With yields averaging 12.7 bushels acreage required
1871	371,000,000	4.15	1,540,000,000	121,000,000
1881	416,000,000	4.38	1,822,000,000	143,000,000
1891	472,600,000	4.50	2,127,000,000	167,000,000
1898	516,500,000	4.50	2,324,000,000	183,000,000
1901	536,100,000	4.50	2,412,000,000	190,000,000
1911	603,700,000	4.50	2,717,000,000	214,000,000
1921	674,000,000	4.50	3,033,000,000	239,000,000
1931	746,100,000	4.50	3,357,000,000	264,000,000
1941	819,200,000	4.50	3,686,000,000	290,000,000

To supply these bread-eaters, the world inhabited by bread-eating populations grew the following quantities of wheat in each of the designated five-year periods :—

TABLE VI.

Years	Bushels—Annual average	Acres—Annual average
1871–75	1,580,000,000, grown on	131,000,000
1876–80	1,746,000,000 ,,	143,000,000
1881–85	1,926,000,000 ,,	152,000,000
1886–90	1,987,000,000 ,,	154,000,000
1891–95	2,201,000,000 ,,	159,000,000

Within the same periods wheat was imported

* The seed quota is kept constant at 0.6 bushel per unit per annum, but the unit food requirements are found to increase in each five-yearly period. There has been a steady increase of unit wheat requirements by reason of the decrease of unit consumption of rye, maslin, spelt, and buckwheat.

from Asia and North Africa by the " bread-eating "
countries as follows :—

TABLE VII.

Years	Bushels—Annual average		Acres—Annual average
1871–75	8,000,000,	the net product of	750,000
1876–80	12,000,000	,, ,,	1,120,000
1881–85	36,000,000	,, ,,	3,360,000
1886–90	39,000,000	,, ,,	3,640,000
1891–95	34,000,000	,, ,,	3,200,000

Broadly speaking, 2,000,000,000 bushels are
now consumed in the countries where they are
grown, either as food or for seed, while the balance
is exported.

That scarcity and high prices have not prevailed
in recent years is due to the fact that since 1889 we
have had seven world crops of wheat and six of
rye abundantly in excess of the average.   These
generous crops increased accumulations to such an
extent as to obscure the fact that the harvests of
1895 and 1896 were each much below current
requirements.   Practically speaking, reserves are
now exhausted, and bread-eaters must be fed from
current harvests—accumulation under present conditions being almost impossible.   This is obvious
from the fact that a harvest equal to that of 1894 (the
greatest crop on record, both in acre-yield and in
the aggregate) would yield less than current needs.

At the present time the disproportion is even higher, owing to unit consumption gradually increasing from year to year, accompanied by slow shrinkage in the wheat area.

TABLE VIII.

	1871	1884	1897	Per cent. of increase or decrease in twenty-six years
Population .	371,000,000	432,800,000	510,000,000	37.5 increase.
Wheat acres	125,800,000	154,300,000	158,000,000	25.6 increase.
Rye acres .	111,000,000	110,300,000	106,500,000	4.1 decrease.

The area planted with the two great bread-making grains is actually less now than thirteen years ago, despite enormous additions to the population. The area under *all* the bread-making grains is absolutely 2.2 per cent. less than thirteen years ago, notwithstanding an increase of one-fifth in requirements for bread.

It is clear we are confronted with a colossal problem that must tax the wits of the wisest. When the bread-eaters have exhausted all possible supplies from the 1897-98 harvest, there will be a deficit of 103,000,000 bushels of wheat, with no substitution possible unless Europeans can be induced to eat Indian corn or rye bread. Up to recent years the growth of wheat has kept pace with demands. As wheat-eaters increased, the acreage under wheat expanded. The world has

become so familiarised with the orderly sequence
of demand and supply, so accustomed to look upon
the vast plains of other wheat-growing countries
as inexhaustible granaries, that, in a light-hearted
way it is taken for granted that so many million
additional acres can be added year after year to the
wheat-growing area of the world. We forget that
the wheat-growing area is of strictly limited extent,
and that a few million acres regularly absorbed
soon mount to a formidable number.

The present position being so gloomy, let us
consider future prospects. What are the capabilities
as regards available area, economic conditions, and
acreage yield of the wheat-growing countries from
whence we now draw our supply?

For the last thirty years the United States have
been the dominant factor in the foreign supply of
wheat, exporting no less than 145,000,000 bushels.
This shows how the bread-eating world has depended, and still depends, on the United States
for the means of subsistence. The entire world's
contributions to the food-bearing area have averaged
but 4,000,000 acres yearly since 1869. It is
scarcely possible that such an average, under
existing conditions, can be doubled for the coming
twenty-five years.

Notwithstanding this expansion, the supplies of

wheat were hardly sufficient for the food demands
of the world. As the area under wheat has increased, that under rye has diminished, with the
result that scarcely an acre has been added to the
world's wheat and rye since 1890 ; and there was
in 1897 a deficit in the 'two principal bread-making
grains of more than 600,000,000 bushels.

Almost yearly, since 1885, additions to the
wheat-growing area have diminished, while the
requirements of the increasing population of
the States have advanced, so that the needed
American supplies have been drawn from the
acreage hitherto used for exportation. Practically
there remains no uncultivated prairie land in the
United States suitable for wheat-growing. The
virgin land has been rapidly absorbed, until at present there is no land left for wheat without reducing
the area for maize, hay, and other necessary crops.

Stocks of wheat and flour in the United States
were, relatively to population, probably never
smaller, if so small as now. The following table
(from *Bradstreet*) shows the visible supply of wheat
in the States on 1st June since 1893 :—

TABLE IX.

	BUSHELS			BUSHELS
1893 . . .	93,700,000		1896 . . .	71,300,000
1894 . . .	80,500,000		1897 . . .	39,200,000
1895 . . .	72,800,000		1898 . . .	32,500,000

It is almost certain that within a generation the

B

ever increasing population of the United States will consume all the wheat grown within its borders, and will be driven to import, and, like ourselves, will scramble for a lion's share of the wheat crop of the world.   This being the outlook, exports of wheat from the United States are only of present interest, and will gradually diminish to a vanishing point.   The enquiry may be restricted to such countries as probably will continue to feed bread-eaters who annually derive a considerable part of their wheat from extraneous sources.*

But if the United States, which grow about one-fifth of the world's wheat, and contribute one-third of all wheat exportations, are even now dropping out of the race, and likely soon to enter the list of wheat-importing countries, what prospect is there that other wheat-growing countries will be able to fill the gap, and by enlarging their acreage under wheat, replace the supply which the States have so long contributed to the world's food?   The withdrawal of 145,000,000 bushels will cause a serious gap in the food supply of wheat-importing countries, and unless this deficit can be met by increased supplies from other countries there will be a dearth for the rest of the world after the British Isles are sufficiently supplied.

Next to the United States, Russia is the

* *See* Note, p. 10.

greatest wheat exporter, supplying nearly 95,000,000 bushels. In 1896 the area under wheat in the Governments of Russia and Poland was 36,000,000 acres. But the yearly consumption of wheat per head during the last ten years has declined 14 per cent., and the consumption of bread is quite 30 per cent. less than is required to keep the population in health. The grain reserved for seed has likewise decreased — the peasantry limiting their sowing with the rise of taxation. The reduction of 14 per cent. in the unit consumption of bread in Russia has added, during the last eighteen years, 1,360,000,000 bushels to the general wheat supply. This factitious excess temporarily staved off scarcity in Europe.

Although Russia at present exports so lavishly, this excess is merely provisional and precarious. The Russian peasant population increases more rapidly than any other in Europe. The yield per acre over European Russia is meagre—not more than 8.6 bushels to the acre—while some authorities consider it as low as 4.6 bushels. The cost of production is low—lower even than on the virgin soils of the United States. The development of the fertile, though somewhat overrated " black earth," which extends across the southern portion of the empire, and beyond the Ural Mountains into

Siberia, progresses rapidly. But, as we have indicated, the consumption of bread in Russia has been reduced to danger point. The peasants starve, and fall
victims to "hunger typhus," whilst the wheat growers
export grain that ought to be consumed at home.*

* This was written in the summer of 1898. What the situation is
in Russia twelve months later may be judged from the following description sent from Moscow, under date 22nd May, and published
in *The Globe* for 26th May 1899 :—

"THE FAMINE IN RUSSIA.

"The Russian public has at last awoke to the fact that there really
is a famine in the land, and money is beginning to flow in from all
sides for the relief of the starving moujiks. The aristocracy is par-
ticularly generous in making donations, and this may perhaps be
ascribed to its former connection with the peasants, their old serfs.
Unfortunately, this sudden outbreak of charity comes all too late.
Even so far back as last autumn one of the leading journals of St
Petersburg drew attention to the fact that there would be a great
famine, and described even then the terrible condition of the peasantry.
As the journal in question was rebuked by the Censor, and partially
suppressed for taking the trouble to speak the truth, few papers dared
to devote much space to the approaching famine. Some papers utterly
ignored it, and, after reading the leading newspapers of Russia, one
remained in happy ignorance of the gaunt spectre of famine already
stalking through the land, and claiming its thousands and tens of
thousands of victims. At last, when the winter was well-nigh past,
the Press summoned up courage, and began to speak in a vague
manner of the failure of the crops in certain parts of Russia, and
allusion was made to the consequent starvation of the people. But
this information came too late, and thousands are now no more whose
lives might have been spared had the full truth of this awful calamity
been published in the autumn instead of towards the close of the
winter.

"As the outside world is still unaware of the enormous extent of
this famine, and of the terrible sufferings of the famine-stricken, I send
you the following extracts from one of the leading Moscow papers :—

"'Every possible sacrifice must be made to aid the distress, which

Considering Siberia as a wheat grower, climate
is the first consideration. Summers are short—as
they are in all regions with continental climates
north of the 45th parallel—and the ripening of

is now at its height. The spring has now come, when the moujiks
need all their energies for their work, and they seem to have lost all
hope and energy. Instead of our rich and powerful " Mother Russia,"
there lies before us a bewitched country teeming with starving beggars.
In travelling from village to village, and in passing from cottage to
cottage, one wonders how human beings can remain human while
living in such a terrible situation. To make matters worse, the
general need does not grow less ; it increases with terrible power.
The aid now being given is altogether insufficient in proportion to the
distress, and reminds one of a jet of water that is being directed on a
house burning on all sides.'

" Letters of this kind are now filling the Press at the eleventh hour,
when the actual state of things was known to thousands in Russia six
months ago. A landowner, who at first made appeals for aid, and is
himself now besieged for help, writes : ' Those who are living far
away cannot believe that all this suffering is so terrible, and that now
on the eve of a great national holiday, the centenary of Pushkine,
which aims at glorifying Russian culture, the value of human life in
Russia has sunk to a few roubles. Yet such is the state of the case.
At the cost of a bottle of champagne it is possible to save several
human lives. If we were even now to make up the total of the
famine-stricken, we should arrive at figures before which no living
soul could fail to be touched.' Some authorities put the number of
starving moujiks at 20,000,000 ; others say the number is far less.
Strange to say, the peasants bear their sufferings with a resignation
worthy of martyrs. ·They regard the famine as being the will of God,
or as a punishment for their sins. Were not this religious spirit of
resignation, the spirit of ' Kismet,' so strongly developed among the
Russian peasantry, the interior of the country would now be the scene
of rapine and revolt. The village priests tell their flocks that it is the
will of God that they should thus starve, or that it is the will of the
saints ; thus the simple, uncomplaining moujik sinks into death
without a murmur on his lips. Life, even at the best, is scarcely
worth living for the majority of Russian peasants.

wheat requires a temperature averaging at least 65°
Fahr. for fifty-five to sixty-five days. As all Siberia
lies north of the summer isotherm of 65°, it follows
that such region is ill adapted to wheat culture
unless some compensation climatic condition exists.
As a fact, the conditions are exceptionally unfavourable in all but very limited districts in the two
westernmost governments. The cultivable lands of
Western Siberia adapted to grain-bearing neither
equal in extent nor in potential productive powers
those of Iowa, Minnesota, and Nebraska. There
are limited tracts of fair productiveness in Central

"The poor sufferers have hit on all kinds of devices in order to
still the pangs of hunger. A friend of mine, who has just visited the
peasants in the government of Kazan, states that the women in one
cottage were in the habit of heating the stove in the evening, and
then of allowing the fumes to spread through the room instead of
escaping properly by the chimney. As a result of this, all the inmates
lost their senses until the morning, and thus the pangs of hunger
were escaped until dawn. The experiment is highly dangerous ; but
the women plead that it is better thus to die in one's sleep than to
perish slowly of hunger. These little devices, which the peasants
relate with an attempt at grim humour, are only too common.

"'Last August,' a correspondent of one of the leading journals of
Moscow writes, 'it was well known that in many districts the land did
not hold out a single hope for the peasantry, and that hundreds of
thousands of people must endure the so-called "half-famine"; that is,
they would receive assistance every month which would enable them
to live for two weeks without starving. The result of this state of
affairs was not long in making itself felt ; the population became
exhausted, and began to die.'

"In the Government of Kazan alone, even in March, there were
more than 10,000 people helplessly ill. But this number is, of course,
much lower than the actual figures, because the doctors were not able

Siberia, and in the valleys of the southern affluents of the Amoor, but these are only just capable of supporting a meagre population.

Prince Hilkoff, Russian Minister of Ways and Communications, declared in 1896 that "Siberia never had produced, and never would produce, wheat and rye enough to feed the Siberian population." And, a year later, Prince Krapotkin backed the statement as substantially correct.

Those who attended the meeting of the British Association last year in Canada must have been struck with the extent and marvellous capacity of

to help the suffering. The 'circuits,' allotted to the country doctors contain often as many as 50,000 persons to be attended by one doctor. The sickness was even greater in the Government of Samara during the last famine. It is, nevertheless, a fact that during the height of the distress, the existence of the last famine was stoutly denied by the *Novce Vremya* the *Grashdanin* and by other leading journals in Russia.

"The peasants are so wretchedly poor for the greater part, that they have not the means to pay for medical attendance ; in consequence, most of the doctors congregate in the towns, and the country districts are thus left practically bare of medical aid. I have known districts containing from 20,000 to 30,000 inhabitants with only one doctor to minister to the wants of thousands of sick persons. Such is the state of the country ; in the towns it is far different, for they contain some of the best doctors and the finest hospitals in the world. It is said that the hospitals of Moscow and St Petersburg are second to none in Europe as regards order, cleanliness, and being up to date in every respect. In the interior of the Empire doctors and hospitals are few and far between. I may say, in conclusion, that the Russian moujik has so far reduced his wants that, as an actual fact, he is now able to exist during the present famine on three or four kopecks a day; in other words, a shilling will keep him alive for about a fortnight."

the fertile plains of Manitoba and the North-West provinces. Here were to be seen 1,290,000 acres of fine wheat-growing land yielding 18,261,950 bushels, one-fifth of which comes to hungry England. Expectations have been cherished that the Canadian North-West would easily supply the world with wheat, and exaggerated estimates are drawn as to the amount of surplus land on which wheat can be grown. Thus far performance has lagged behind promise, the wheat-bearing area of all Canada having increased less than 500,000 acres since 1884, while the exports have not increased in greater proportion. As the wheat area of Manitoba and the North-West has increased, the wheat area of Ontario and the Eastern provinces has decreased, the added acres being little more than sufficient to meet the growing requirements of population. We have seen calculations showing that Canada contains 500,000,000 acres of profitable wheat land. The impossibility of such an estimate ever being fulfilled will be apparent when it is remembered that the whole area employed in both temperate zones for growing all the staple food crops is not more than 580,000,000 acres, and that in no country has more than 9 per cent. of the area been devoted to wheat culture.

The most trustworthy estimates give Canada a wheat area of not more than 6,000,000 acres in the next twelve years, increasing to a maximum of 12,000,000 acres in twenty-five years. The development of this promising area necessarily must be slow, since prairie land cannot be laid under wheat in advance of a population sufficient to supply the needful labour at seed time and harvest. As population increases so do home demands for wheat.

The net exports average 8,970,000 bushels yearly, being 24.3 per cent. of the net product.*

The fertility of the North-West provinces of the Dominion is due to an exceptional and curious circumstance. In winter the ground freezes to a considerable depth. Wheat is sown in the spring, generally April, when the frozen ground has been thawed to a depth of 3 inches. Under the hot sun of the short summer the grain sprouts with surprising rapidity, partly because the roots are

* TABLE X.

Acreage, Crop, and Exports of Wheat from Canada from 1891 to 1896 :—

Year	Population	Acres	Total bushels	Bushels exported
1891	4,833,000	2,690,000	62,600,000	3,000,000
1892	4,885,000	2,910,000	49,700,000	10,200,000
1893	4,936,000	2,800,000	42,700,000	11,000,000
1894	4,986,000	2,550,000	44,600,000	11,000,000
1895	5,040,000	2,560,000	57,500,000	9,200,000
1896	5,090,000	2,700,000	40,800,000	10,400,000
1897	5,140,000	2,900,000	56,600,000	8,000,000

supplied with water from the thawing depths. The summer is too short to thaw the ground thoroughly, and gate-posts or other dead wood extracted in autumn are found still frozen at their lower ends.

Australasia, as a potential contributor to the world's supply of wheat, affords another fertile field for speculation. Climatic conditions limit the Australian wheat area to a small portion of the southern littoral belt. Professor Shelton considers there are still 50,000,000 acres in Queensland suitable for wheat, but hitherto it has never had more than 150,000 acres under cultivation. Crops in former days were liable to rust, but since the Rust in Wheat conferences, and the dissemination of instruction to farmers, rust no longer has any terrors. I am informed by the Queensland Department of Agriculture that of late years they practically have bred wheat vigorous enough to resist this plague. For the second season in succession the wheat crop last year was destroyed over large areas in Victoria ; and in South Australia the harvest averaged not more than about $3\frac{3}{4}$ bushels per acre after meeting Colonial requirements for food and seed, leaving only 684,000 bushels for export. In most other districts the yield falls to such an extent as to cause Europeans to wonder why the pursuit of wheat-raising is continued.

New Zealand has a moist climate resembling that of central and southern England, while South Australia is semi-arid, resembling Western Kansas. Only two countries in the world yield as much wheat per acre as New Zealand — these are Denmark and the United Kingdom. Notwithstanding the great yield of wheat, due to an equable climate, New Zealand finds fruit and dairy farming still more profitable. The climatic conditions favourable to wheat are also conducive to luxuriant growths of nutritious grasses. Thus the New Zealander ships his butter more than half-way round the world, and competes successfully with Western Europe.

During the last twenty-seven years the Austro-Hungarian population has increased 21.8 per cent. as against an increase of 54.6 per cent. in the acreage of wheat. Notwithstanding this disparity in the rates of increase, exports have practically ceased by reason of an advance of nearly 80 per cent. in unit consumption. There can be little doubt that Austro-Hungary is about to enter the ranks of importing nations, although in Hungary a considerable area of wheat land remains to be brought under cultivation.

The land under wheat in Austro-Hungary, according to the latest official figures, is 11,000,000

acres.   The 1897-98 crop, including that of
Croatia-Slavonia, is 55,000,000 bushels below
that of 1896-97, and as exports during the last
five years have averaged less than 4,000,000
bushels per annum, the imports of wheat are
expected to be large.

Roumania is an important wheat-growing country.
In 1896 it produced 69,000,000 bushels, and
exported 34,000,000 bushels.   It has a considerable
amount of surplus land which can be used for
wheat, although for many years the wheat area is
not likely to exceed home requirements.

France comes next to the United States as a
producer of wheat; but for our purpose she counts
but little, being dependent on supplies from abroad
for an average quantity of 14 per cent. of her own
production.   There is practically no spare land in
France that can be put under wheat in sufficient
quantity to enable her to do more than provide for
increase of population.

Germany is a gigantic importer of wheat, her
imports rising 700 per cent. in the last twenty-five
years, and now averaging 35,000,000 bushels.
Other nations of Europe, also importers, do not
require detailed mention, as under no conceivable
conditions would they be able to do more than
supply wheat for the increasing requirements of

their local population, and, instead of replenishing, would probably diminish, the world's stores.

The prospective supply of wheat from Argentina and Uruguay has been greatly overrated. The agricultural area includes less than 100,000,000 acres of good, bad, and indifferent land, much of which is best adapted for pastoral purposes. There is no prospect of Argentina ever being able to devote more than 30,000,000 acres to wheat; the present wheat area is about 6,000,000 acres, an area that may be doubled in the next twelve years. But the whole arable region is subject to great climatic vicissitudes, and to frosts that ravage the fields south of the 37th parallel. Years of systematised energy are frustrated in a few days—perhaps hours—by a single cruelty of Nature, such as a plague of locusts, a tropical rain, or a devastating hail storm. It will take years to bring the surplus lands of Argentina into cultivation, and the population is even now insufficient to supply labour at seed time and harvest.

During the next twelve years, Uruguay may add 1,000,000 acres to the world's wheat fields; but social, political, and economic conditions seriously interfere with agricultural development.

At the present time South Africa is an importer of wheat, and the regions suitable to cereals do not

exceed a few million acres. Great expectations
have been formed as to the fertility of Mashonaland,
the Shire Highlands, and the Kikuyu plateau, and
as to the adaptation of these regions to the growth
of wheat. But wheat culture fails where the
banana ripens, and the banana flourishes throughout Central Africa, except in limited areas of great
elevation. In many parts of Africa insect pests
render it impossible to store grain, and without
grain-stores there can be little hope of large
exports.

North Africa, formerly the granary of Rome,
now exports less than 5,000,000 bushels of wheat
annually, and these exports are on the decline,
owing to increased home demands. With scientific
irrigation, Egypt could supply three times her
present amount of wheat, although no increase is
likely unless the cotton fields of the Delta are
diverted to grain growing. In Algeria and Tunis
nearly all reclaimed lands are devoted to the
production of wine, for which a brisk demand
exists. Were this land devoted to the growth of
wheat, an additional 5,000,000 bushels might be
obtained.

The enormous acreage devoted to wheat in
India has been declining for some years, and in
1895 over 20,000,000 acres yielded 185,000,000

bushels. Seven-eighths of this harvest is required for native consumption, and only one-eighth on an average is available for export. The annual increase of population is more than 3,000,000, demanding an addition to the food-bearing lands of not less than 1,800,000 acres annually. In recent years the increase has been less than one-fourth of this amount.*

In surveying the limitations and vicissitudes of wheat crops, I have endeavoured to keep free from exaggeration, and have avoided insistence on doubtful points. I have done my best to get trustworthy facts and figures, but from the nature of the case it is impossible to attain complete accuracy. Great caution is required in sifting the numerous varying current statements respecting the estimated areas and total produce of wheat throughout the world. The more closely official

---

* So long ago as 16th April 1891, the following statement, by a leading Indian economist, appeared in the *Daily Englishman* of Calcutta : "People do not realise the fact that all the wheat India produces is required for home consumption, and that this fact is not likely to be realised until a serious disaster occurs, and that even now less than 9 per cent. is exported. It is a self-evident fact that a slight expansion of consumption, or a partial failure of crops of other food grains, will be sufficient to absorb the small proportion now exported. Besides, we have a steady increase of consumption, in consequence of the natural growth of the population, as well as in the gradual improvement of the condition of a considerable part of the people in the cities. I believe that, comparatively speaking, India will in a few years cease to export wheat, and soon thereafter become an importing country."

estimates are examined, the more defective are they found, and comparatively few figures are sufficiently well established to bear the deductions often drawn. In doubtful cases I have applied to the highest authorities in each country, and in the case of conflicting accounts have taken data the least favourable to sensational or panic-engendering statements. In a few instances of accurate statistics their value is impaired by age; but for 95 per cent. of my figures I quote good authorities, while for the remaining 5 per cent. I rely on the best commercial estimates derived from the appearance of the growing crops, the acreage under cultivation, and the yield last year. The maximum probable error would make no appreciable difference in my argument.

The facts and figures I have set before you are easily interpreted. Since 1871 unit consumption of wheat, including seed, has slowly increased in the United Kingdom to the present amount of 6 bushels per head per annum; while the rate of consumption for seed and food by the whole world of bread-eaters was 4.15 bushels per unit per annum for the eight years ending 1878, and at the present time is 4.5 bushels. Under present conditions of low - acre yield, wheat cannot long retain its dominant position among the food-stuffs of the civilised world. The details of the impending catastrophe no one can predict, but its general direction is obvious enough. Should all the wheat-growing countries add to their area to the utmost capacity, on the most careful calculation the yield would give us only an addition of some 100,000,000 acres, supplying at the average world-yield of 12.7 bushels to the acre, 1,270,000,000 bushels, just enough to supply the increase of population among bread-eaters till the year 1931.*

At the present time there exists a deficit in the wheat area of 31,000 square miles—a deficit masked by the fact that the ten world crops of wheat harvested in the ten years ending 1896 were more than 5 per cent. above the average of the previous twenty-six years.

When provision shall have been made, if possible, to feed 230,000,000 units likely to be added to the bread-eating populations by 1931— by the complete occupancy of the arable areas of the temperate zone now partially occupied—where can be grown the additional 330,000,000 bushels of

---

* An average wheat crop on the 1897-98 acreage would be 2,070,000,000 bushels. Adding to this 1,270,000,000 bushels, makes a grand total of 3,340,000,000 bushels. But the estimate on page 13 shows that in the year 1931 the bread-eaters will require 3,357,000,000 bushels. Thus there will be in 1931 a deficiency of 17,000,000 bushels, unless the average yield per acre be increased.

c

wheat required ten years later by a hungry world?
What is to happen if the present rate of population
be maintained, and if arable areas of sufficient extent
cannot be adapted and made contributory to the
subsistence of so great a host?

Are we to go hungry, and to know the trial of
scarcity? That is the poignant question. Thirty
years is but a day in the life of a nation. Those
present who may attend the meeting of the British
Association thirty years hence will judge how far
my forecasts are justified.

If bread fails—not only us, but all the bread-
eaters of the world—what are we to do? We are
born wheat-eaters. Other races, vastly superior to
us in numbers, but differing widely in material and
intellectual progress, are eaters of Indian corn, rice,
millet, and other grains; but none of these
grains have the food value, the concentrated,
health-sustaining power of wheat, and it is on
this account that the accumulated experience of
civilised mankind has set wheat apart as the fit
and proper food for the development of muscle and
brains.

It is said that when other wheat-exporting
countries realise that the States can no longer
keep pace with the demand, these countries will
extend their area of cultivation, and struggle to

keep up the supply *pari passu* with the falling off in other quarters. But will this comfortable and cherished doctrine bear the test of examination?

Cheap production of wheat depends on a variety of causes, varying greatly in different countries. Taking the cost of producing a given quantity of wheat in the United Kingdom at 100s., the cost for the same amount in the United States is 67s., in India 66s., and in Russia 54s. We require cheap labour, fertile soil, easy transportation to market, low taxation and rent, and no export or import duties. Labour will rise in price, and fertility diminish as the requisite manurial constituents in the virgin soil become exhausted. Facility of transportation to market will be aided by railways, but these are slow and costly to construct, and it will not pay to carry wheat by rail beyond a certain distance. These considerations show that the price of wheat tends to increase. On the other hand, the artificial impediments of taxation and customs duties tend to diminish as demand increases and prices rise.

I have said that starvation may be averted through the laboratory. Before we are in the grip of actual dearth the Chemist will step in and postpone the day of famine to so distant a period that we, and our sons and grandsons, may legitimately live without undue solicitude for the future.

It is now recognised that all crops require what is called a "dominant" manure. Some need nitrogen, some potash, others phosphates. Wheat pre-eminently demands nitrogen, fixed in the form of ammonia or nitric acid. All other necessary constituents exist in the soil; but nitrogen is mainly of atmospheric origin, and is rendered "fixed" by a slow and precarious process which requires a combination of rare meteorological and geographical conditions to enable it to advance at a sufficiently rapid rate to become of commercial importance.

There are several sources of available nitrogen. The distillation of coal in the process of gas-making yields a certain amount of its nitrogen in the form of ammonia; and this product, as sulphate of ammonia, is a substance of considerable commercial value to gas companies. But the quantity produced is comparatively small; all Europe does not yield more than 400,000 annual tons, and, in view of the unlimited nitrogen required to substantially increase the world's wheat crop, this slight amount of coal ammonia is not of much significance. For a long time guano has been one of the most important sources of nitrogenous manures, but guano deposits are so near exhaustion that they may be dismissed from consideration.

Much has been said of late years, and many hopes raised by the discovery of Hellriegel and Wilfarth, that leguminous plants bear on their roots nodosities abounding in bacteria endowed with the property of fixing atmospheric nitrogen ; and it is proposed that the necessary amount of nitrogen demanded by grain crops should be supplied to the soil by cropping it with clover and ploughing in the plant when its nitrogen assimilation is complete. But it is questionable whether such a mode of procedure will lead to the lucrative stimulation of crops. It must be admitted that practice has long been ahead of science, and for ages farmers have valued and cultivated leguminous crops. The four - course rotation is turnips, barley, clover, wheat — a sequence popular more than two thousand years ago. On the Continent, in certain localities, there has been some extension of microbe cultivation ; at home we have not reached even the experimental stage. Our present knowledge leads to the conclusion that the much more frequent growth of clover on the same land, even with successful microbe - seeding and proper mineral supplies, would be attended with uncertainty and difficulties. The land soon becomes what is called "clover sick," and turns barren.

There is still another and invaluable source of fixed nitrogen. I mean the treasure locked up in the sewage and drainage of our towns. Individually the amount so lost is trifling, but multiply the loss by the number of inhabitants, and we have the startling fact that, in the United Kingdom, we are content to hurry down our drains and water-courses, into the sea, fixed nitrogen to the value of no less than £16,000,000 per annum. This unspeakable waste continues, and no effective and universal method is yet contrived of converting sewage into corn. Of this barbaric waste of manurial constituents Liebig, nearly half a century ago, wrote in these prophetic words: "Nothing will more certainly consummate the ruin of England than a scarcity of fertilisers—it means a scarcity of food. It is impossible that such a sinful violation of the divine laws of Nature should for ever remain unpunished; and the time will probably come for England sooner than for any other country, when, with all her wealth in gold, iron, and coal, she will be unable to buy one-thousandth part of the food which she has, during hundreds of years, thrown recklessly away."

The more widely this wasteful system is extended, recklessly returning to the sea what we have taken from the land, the more surely and quickly will the finite stocks of nitrogen locked up in the soils of the world become exhausted. Let us remember that the plant creates nothing; there is nothing in bread which is not absorbed from the soil, and unless the abstracted nitrogen is returned to the soil, its fertility must ultimately be exhausted. When we apply to the land nitrate of soda, sulphate of ammonia, or guano, we are drawing on the earth's capital, and our drafts will not perpetually be honoured. Already we see that a virgin soil cropped for several years loses its productive powers, and without artificial aid becomes infertile. Thus the strain to meet demands is increasingly great. Witness the yield of 40 bushels of wheat per acre under favourable conditions, dwindling through exhaustion of soil to less than 7 bushels of poor grain, and the urgency of husbanding the limited store of fixed nitrogen becomes apparent. The store of nitrogen in the atmosphere is practically unlimited, but it is fixed and rendered assimilable by plants only by cosmic processes of extreme slowness. The nitrogen which with a light heart we liberate in a battleship broadside, has taken millions of minute organisms patiently working for centuries to win from the atmosphere.*

The only available compound containing sufficient fixed nitrogen to be used on a world-wide scale as a nitrogenous manure is nitrate of soda, or Chili saltpetre. This substance occurs native over a narrow band of the plain of Tamarugal, in the northern provinces of Chili between the Andes and the coast hills. In this rainless district, for countless ages, the continuous fixation of atmospheric nitrogen by the soil, its conversion into nitrate by the slow transformation of billions of nitrifying organisms, its combination with soda, and the crystallisation of the nitrate have been steadily proceeding, until the nitrate fields of Chili have become of vast commercial importance, and promise to be of inestimably greater value in the future. The growing exports of nitrate from Chili at present amount to about 1,200,000 tons.

At the present time the contributory areas †

---

* Sir Andrew Noble informs me that a first-class battleship would carry about 63 tons of cordite, and we may suppose that in a general action 40 tons of this would be expended. Now, at Trafalgar, Nelson had twenty-seven line-of-battleships, and the allied forces thirty-three. If we suppose a similar number of modern battleships and first-class cruisers to be engaged, and each to expend 40 tons of cordite, the total volume of nitrogen set free would be 302,400 cubic metres, or about 380 tons, equivalent to 2,300 tons of nitrate of soda.

† See Note, p. 10.

devoted to the world's growth of wheat are about 163,000,000 acres. These do not include some 40,000,000 acres in India, Persia, Turkey in Asia, and North Africa. At the average of 12.7 bushels per acre this gives 2,070,000,000 bushels. But thirty years hence the demand will be 3,260,000,000 bushels, and there will be difficulty in finding the necessary acreage on which to grow the additional amount required. By increasing the present yield per acre from 12.7 to 20 bushels we should, with our present acreage, secure a crop of the requisite amount. Now, from 12.7 to 20 bushels per acre is a moderate increase of productiveness, and there is no doubt that a dressing with nitrate of soda will give this increase and more.

The action of nitrate of soda in improving the yield of wheat has been studied practically by Sir John Lawes and Sir Henry Gilbert on their ex-perimental field at Rothamstead. This field was sown with wheat for thirteen consecutive years without manure, and yielded an average of 11.9 bushels to the acre. For the next thirteen years it was sown with wheat, and dressed with 5 cwt. of nitrate of soda per acre, other mineral constituents also being present. The average yield for these years was 36.4 bushels per acre—an increase of 24.5 bushels. In other words, 22.86 lbs. of nitrate of soda produce an increase of one bushel of wheat.

At this rate, to increase the world's crop of wheat by 7.3 bushels, about 1½ cwt. of nitrate of soda must annually be applied to each acre. The amount required to raise the world's crop on 163,000,000 acres from the present supply of 2,070,000,000 bushels to the required 3,260,000,000 bushels will be 12,000,000 tons, distributed in vary-ing amounts over the wheat-growing countries of the world. The countries which produce more than the average of 12.7 bushels will require less, and those below the average will require more; but, broadly speaking, about 12,000,000 tons annually of nitrate of soda will be required, in addition to the 1,250,000 tons already absorbed by the world.

It is difficult to get trustworthy estimates of the amount of nitrate surviving in the nitre beds. Common rumour declares the supply to be inex-haustible, but cautious local authorities state that at the present rate of export, of over 1,000,000 tons per annum, the raw material "caliche," con-taining from 25 to 50 per cent. nitrate, will be exhausted in from twenty to thirty years.

Dr Newton, who has spent years on the nitrate fields, tells me there is a lower class material, con-taining a small proportion of nitrate, which cannot at present be used, but which may ultimately be manufactured at a profit. Apart from a few of the more scientific manufacturers, no one is sanguine enough to think this debatable material will ever be worth working. If we assume a liberal estimate for nitrate obtained from the lower grade deposit, and say that it will equal in quantity that from the richer quality, the supply may last, possibly, fifty years, at the rate of 1,000,000 tons a year; but, at the rate required to augment the world's supply of wheat to the point demanded thirty years hence, it will not last more than four years.

I have passed in review all the wheat-growing countries of the world, with the exception of those whose united supplies are so small as to make little appreciable difference to the argument. The situation may be summed up briefly thus: The world's demand for wheat—the leading bread-stuff —increases in a crescendo ratio year by year. Gradually all the wheat-bearing land on the globe is appropriated to wheat-growing, until we are within measurable distance of using the last available acre. We must then rely on nitrogenous manures to increase the fertility of the land under wheat, so as to raise the yield from the world's low average—12.7 bushels per acre—to a higher average. To do this efficiently, and feed the bread-

eaters for a few years, will exhaust all the available
store of nitrate of soda. For years past we have
been spending fixed nitrogen at a culpably ex-
travagant rate, heedless of the fact that it is fixed
with extreme slowness and difficulty, while its
liberation in the free state takes place always with
rapidity, and sometimes with explosive violence.

Some years ago Mr Stanley Jevons uttered a
note of warning as to the near exhaustion of our
British coal-fields. But the exhaustion of the world's
stock of fixed nitrogen is a matter of far greater
importance. It means not only a catastrophe little
short of starvation for the wheat-eaters, but, in-
directly, scarcity for those who exist on inferior
grains, together with a lower standard of living for
meat-eaters, scarcity of mutton and beef, and even
the extinction of gunpowder!

There is a gleam of light amid this darkness of
despondency. In its free state nitrogen is one of
the most abundant and pervading bodies on the
face of the earth. Every square yard of the earth's
surface has nitrogen gas pressing down on it to the
extent of about 7 tons—but this is in the *free*
state, and wheat demands it *fixed*. To convey this
idea in an object-lesson, I may tell you that, previous
to its destruction by fire, Colston Hall, measuring
146 feet by 80 feet by 70 feet, contained 27 tons'

weight of nitrogen in its atmosphere ; it also contained one-third of a ton of argon. In the free
gaseous state this nitrogen is worthless ; combined
in the form of nitrate of soda it would be worth
about £2000.

For years past attempts have been made to effect
the fixation of atmospheric nitrogen, and some of
the processes have met with sufficient partial
success to warrant experimentalists in pushing their
trials still further ; but I think I am right in saying
that no process has yet been brought to the notice
of scientific or commercial men which can be considered successful either as regards cost or yield of
product. It is possible, by several methods, to fix a
certain amount of atmospheric nitrogen ; but to the
best of my knowledge no process has hitherto con-
verted more than a small amount, and this at a cost
largely in excess of the present market value of
fixed nitrogen.

The fixation of atmospheric nitrogen therefore is
one of the great discoveries awaiting the ingenuity
of chemists. It is certainly deeply important in
its practical bearings on the future welfare and
happiness of the civilised races of mankind. This
unfulfilled problem, which so far has eluded the
strenuous attempts of those who have tried to wrest
the secret from nature, differs materially from other

chemical discoveries which are in the air, so to speak, but are not yet matured. The fixation of nitrogen is vital to the progress of civilised humanity. Other discoveries minister to our increased intellectual comfort, luxury, or convenience ; they serve to make life easier, to hasten the acquisition of wealth, or to save time, health, or worry. The fixation of nitrogen is a question of the not far-distant future. Unless we can class it among certainties to come, the great Caucasian race will cease to be foremost in the world, and will be squeezed out of existence by races to whom wheaten bread is not the staff of life.

Let me see if it is not possible even now to solve the momentous problem. As far back as 1892 I exhibited, at one of the Soirées of the Royal Society, an experiment on " The Flame of Burning Nitrogen." I showed that nitrogen is a combustible gas, and the reason why when once ignited the flame does not spread through the atmosphere and deluge the world in a sea of nitric acid is, that its igniting point is higher than the temperature of its flame—not, therefore, hot enough to set fire to the adjacent mixture. But by passing a strong induction current between terminals the air takes fire, and continues to burn with a powerful flame, producing nitrous and nitric acids. This inconsiderable experiment may not unlikely lead to the development of a mighty industry destined to solve the great food problem. With the object of burning out nitrogen from air so as to leave argon behind, Lord Rayleigh fitted up apparatus for performing the operation on a larger scale, and succeeded in effecting the union of 29.4 grammes of mixed nitrogen and oxygen at an expenditure of one horse-power. Following these figures it would require one Board of Trade unit to form 74 grammes of nitrate of soda, and therefore 14,000 units to form 1 ton. To generate electricity in the ordinary way with steam engines and dynamos, it is now possible, with a steady load night and day, and engines working at maximum efficiency, to produce current at a cost of one-third of a penny per Board of Trade unit. At this rate 1 ton of nitrate of soda would cost £26. But electricity from coal and steam engines is too costly for large industrial purposes ; at Niagara, where water power is used, electricity can be sold at a profit for one-seventeenth of a penny per Board of Trade unit. At this rate nitrate of soda would cost not more than £5 per ton. But the limit of cost is not yet reached, and it must be remembered that the initial data are derived from small scale experiments, in which the object was not economy, but rather to demonstrate the practicability of the com-

bustion method, and to utilise it for isolating argon.
Even now electric nitrate at £5 a ton compares
favourably with Chili nitrate at £7, 10s. a ton; and
all experience shows that when the road has been
pointed out by a small laboratory experiment, the
industrial operations that may follow are always
conducted at a cost considerably lower than could
be anticipated from the laboratory figures.

Before we decide that electric nitrate is a commercial possibility, a final question must be mooted.
We are dealing with wholesale figures, and must
take care that we are not simply shifting difficulties
a little further back without really diminishing them.
We start with a shortage of wheat, and the natural
remedy is to put more land under cultivation. As
the land cannot be stretched, and there is so much
of it and no more, the object is to render the available area more productive by a dressing with nitrate
of soda. But nitrate of soda is limited in quantity,
and will soon be exhausted. Human ingenuity can
contend even with these apparently hopeless difficulties. Nitrate can be produced artificially by the
combustion of the atmosphere. Here we come to
finality in one direction; our stores are inex-
haustible. But how about electricity? Can we
generate enough energy to produce 12,000,000 tons
of nitrate of soda annually? A preliminary calcula-

tion shows that there need be no fear on that score ; Niagara alone is capable of supplying the required electric energy without much lessening its mighty flow.

The future can take care of itself. The artificial production of nitrate is clearly within view, and by its aid the land devoted to wheat can be brought up to the 30 bushels per acre standard. In days to come, when the demand may again overtake supply, we may safely leave our successors to grapple with the stupendous food problem.

And, in the next generation, instead of trusting mainly to food-stuffs which flourish in temperate climates, we probably shall trust more and more to the exuberant food-stuffs of the tropics, where, instead of one yearly sober harvest, jeopardised by any shrinkage of the scanty days of summer weather, or of the few steady inches of rainfall, Nature annually supplies heat and water enough to ripen two or three successive crops of food-stuffs in extraordinary abundance. To mention one plant alone, Humboldt—from what precise statistics I know not—computed that, acre for acre, the food-productiveness of the banana is 133 times that of wheat—the unripe banana, before its starch is converted into sugar, is said to make excellent bread.

Considerations like these must in the end

D

determine the range and avenues of commerce, perhaps the fate of continents. We must develop and guide Nature's latent energies, we must utilise her inmost workshops, we must call into commercial existence Central Africa and Brazil to redress the balance of Odessa and Chicago.

REPLIES TO MY CRITICS

II

SINCE the delivery of this foregoing Presidential Address to the British Association, many criticisms—and not a few of them adverse—have appeared in the Press. To reply to my critics individually would be impossible, so I take the collective method of dealing with the most prominent objectors, and place thus before the members of the British Association, and the scientific public at large, the facts and reasons upon which my contested statements were founded.

I START with a widely circulated pamphlet by Mr Edward Atkinson, of Boston, U.S.A.

In an important section of my Address I referred to the part taken by the United States in the world's wheat supply, and to the possibility that the capacity of the States for exportation at no distant date will be reduced and ultimately cease altogether. But it is affirmed by Mr Atkinson *that the United States of America could supply the whole world's demand for wheat !* and that the Republic would be ready to contract for the supply of the United Kingdom for the next thirty years provided we would offer a dollar a bushel in Mark Lane as a permanent price!

Mr Atkinson quotes, apparently with irony, my estimate of the wheat crop of 1897-98 at 1,921,000,000 bushels; but he omits to notice—as *Beerbohm* and others have done—that my estimates referred to what I have called "the contributory area," and not to the entire world.

That my estimate was as correct as such an estimate can be is shown by the fact that the very latest computations, based on final official returns respecting 85 per cent. of the total quantity, make the amount 1,899,000,000 bushels. Moreover, a tabulation in Broomhall's *Corn Trade News* of 20th September 1898, places the output of the regions I so clearly designated at 1,987,000,000 bushels! Even so adverse a critic of my Address as *Beerbohm* furnishes proof of its accuracy; as, in its issue of 7th December 1898, it makes, in a table of six world crops, the 1897-98 outputs of "the con-tributory areas" but 1,954,800,000 bushels, although, in so doing, it adds some 59,000,000 bushels to the official estimates of the crops of and the United States! Reducing the American and Roumanian crops to official terms, *Beerbohm's* total is remarkably close to mine. Variation from official returns appears in relation to the outputs of many countries in the tabulation of world crops in *Beerbohm* of 7th December, and we ought not to be surprised that it occurs in relation to the crops of such distant countries as America and Roumania, especially when it is found that the quantities therein credited to the United Kingdom for the five years preceding 1898 vary from Major Craigie's official determinations in amounts ranging from 247,000 bushels in 1896 to more than 1,500,000 bushels in 1894. Even *Beerbohm's* totals for the respective world crops are such as to require reservation in their acceptance, because of the defective summation; that for 1894 alone being reduced 12,800,000 bushels by such a defect, in addition to more than 1,500,000 bushels by reason of an under-statement of the crop of our own country.

Mr Atkinson next quotes my statement that :—

" Bread-eaters have almost eaten up the reserves of wheat, and the 1897 harvest being under average, the conditions become serious."

It is a pity the related portion of the paragraph
was omitted, for it thus continues :—

"That scarcity and high prices have not prevailed in
recent years is due to the fact that since 1889 we have had
seven world crops of wheat and six of rye abundantly in
excess of the average. These generous crops increased
accumulations to such an extent as to obscure the fact
that the harvests of 1895 and 1896 were each much below
current requirements. Practically speaking, reserves are
now exhausted, and bread-eaters must be fed from current
harvests — accumulation under present conditions being
almost impossible. This is obvious from the fact that a
harvest equal to that of 1894 (the greatest crop on record,
both in acre-yield and in the aggregate) would yield less
than current needs."

Had the entire paragraph been quoted, and had
Mr Atkinson supplemented the quotation with my
tabular statements, showing the acres employed,
average yields per acre, the aggregate yearly output in all the regions named in the Address as
occupied by bread-eaters of the Caucasian race, and
the annual imports of such regions from Asia and
North Africa for each of the seven years ending
with 1896, he would have enabled the reader to
judge as to the degree of credit to which the
statement in relation to the seven crops in question
was entitled.

That the reader may see what degree of credence

should be accorded to the statements in that portion of the Address which Mr Atkinson only quoted in part, I append a numerical table showing the acreage employed, the yield per acre, the product of each year from such acreage in the countries inhabited by bread-eating races as designated in the first quotation given above. It should be noted that this statement in relation to the crops harvested in the seven years ending with 1896, is not intended to refer to the entire world, or any part of it other than the countries inhabited by the designated populations of Caucasian race.

TABLE XI.

Wheat Acreage, Yield, and Product of Countries Inhabited by Bread-eating Populations of Caucasian Race.

Year	Acres	Yield per acre	Wheat grown	Per cent. of yield an acre in excess of a 26 years' average	Wheat imported from Asia and North Africa
			Bushels		Bushels
1890	156,700,000	12.78	2,003,000,000	0.6 +	33,000,000
1891	158,300,000	12.92	2,045,000,000	1.7 +	66,000,000
1892	161,900,000	13.34	2,159,000,000	5.0 +	34,000,000
1893	159,100,000	13.53	2,153,000 000	6.5 +	26,000,000
1894	159,800,000	14.19	2,268,000,000	11.7 +	20,000,000
1895	158,100,000	13.69	2,165,000,000	7.8 +	23,000,000
1896	158,000,000	13.58	2,146,000,000	6.9 +	15,000,000
TOTALS	1,111,900,000	13.44	14,939,000,000	5.8 +	217,000,000

NOTE.—Wheat grown and imported constitute food and seed supply of the designated bread-eating populations.

The countries covered by the above table having given yields averaging 12.7 bushels an acre, during a period of twenty-six years, ending with 1896, it follows that the supply of the last seven years was some 823,000,000 bushels more than it would have been with no better than average acre-yields from the seven harvests.

Quoting that paragraph of the Address in which I stated that :—

"Practically there remains no uncultivated prairie land in the United States suitable for wheat-growing. The virgin land has been rapidly absorbed, until at present there is no land left for wheat without reducing the area for maize, hay, and other necessary crops."

Mr Atkinson remarks that, " It is difficult for a citizen of the United States, who has given any attention to the potential of our land, to conceive of such views being held by an Englishman of highest scientific intelligence."

Mr Atkinson proceeds to say that :—

"The point to which I wish to direct attention and enquiry is this alleged nearly complete taking up of the land of the United States capable of producing wheat in paying quantities. The question which Sir William Crookes puts is this : He says there is a deficit in the wheat area of 31,000 square miles, which must be con-verted to wheat-growing in order to keep up with the in-creasing demand of the world to prevent wheat starvation."

It will be seen that here we have a misconception of my language and apprehension, as Mr
Atkinson couples the reference to a deficit of 31,000
square miles to his declared intention to enquire
specifically into the alleged nearly complete occupa-
tion of the wheat lands of the United States. He
conveys the erroneous impression that I had stated
the existence of a deficit of 31,000 square miles
in the wheat area of the United States that could
only be made good by conversions which, it is
implied, I proposed. What I did say, referring
to *all the countries* inhabited by bread-eating populations, was :—

" At the present time there exists a deficit in the wheat
area of 31,000 square miles—a deficit masked by the fact
that the ten world crops of wheat harvested in the ten
years ending 1896 were more than 5 per cent. above the
average of the previous twenty-six years."

Nowhere in the Address is there an intimation
that the deficit was limited to the United States,
nor did I propose to convert maize lands to wheat-
fields, or to convert the stated deficit to wheat-
growing or to anything else. The only reference to
maize lands that can be even twisted into a proposal
of such conversion was the statement that, in the
United States " there is no land left for wheat without reducing the area for maize, hay, and other

necessary crops." This I said to notify how
complete was the exhaustion of available wheat
lands in that country.

The existing deficit of some 31,000 square miles
in the wheat areas of the entire bread-eating world
might be neutralised by adding to such areas
20,000,000 acres of new wheat-bearing lands, but
this would not be a *conversion of a deficit to wheat-
growing*. Such a disposition of a deficit is incon-
ceivable; a deficit is not a material thing, it lacks
tangibility to render it convertible.

The position assumed in the Address, having
reference to the magnitude of requirements compared
to the world's remaining available wheat lands, was
that all the potentially wheat-bearing prairie of the
United States had practically been brought into use,
and that there could be no material expansion of the
wheat area of that country otherwise than by *reducing* the areas required for the production of maize,
hay, and other crops equally essential to national
well-being as wheat.

There are, however, citizens of the United States
—when wheat was bringing the lowest price of the
last 300 years—who were ready to state that maize
and other fields would be converted into wheat-
bearing lands as soon as the price for wheat became
relatively higher than prices for other grains. That

such forecasts were not erroneous is evident from changes in crop distribution as shown in the following table (which includes only data from the U.S. Department of Agriculture), indicating that there is fair reason to believe that no land is left for wheat-growing without *reducing* the areas under maize, hay, and other necessary crops.

TABLE XII.

Crop Distribution of the Primary Food Staples of the United States in 1889, 1895, and 1898.

	YEARS			Change since 1895	Percentage of Change
	1889	1895	1898		
	Acres	Acres	Acres	Acres	
Maize .	78,300,000	82,100,000	77,700,000	4,400,000 –	5.4 –
Wheat .	38,100,000	34,000,000	44,100,000	10,100,000 +	29.7 +
Oats . ' .	27,500,000	27,900,000	25,800,000	2,100,000 –	7.5 –
Barley .	3,000,000	3,000,000	2,600,000	400,000 –	13.3 –
Rye . .	2,400,000	1,900,000	1,600,000	300,000 –	15.8 –
Buckwheat	900,000	800,000	700,000	100,000 –	12.5 –
Potatoes .	2,600,000	3,000,000	2,600,000	400,000 –	13.3 –
TOTALS .	152,800,000	152,700,000	155,100,000	2,400,000 +	1.6 +
Net increase of primary food areas in nine years				2,300,000 +	1.5 +

This table reveals a remarkable constancy in the total of food areas, and shows that in the last nine years additions have equalled but $1\frac{1}{2}$ of 1 per cent. of the total; yet nine years ago wheat was bringing—as it did every year up to and including 1892—a yearly average of more than the required 33s. a quarter, for average grades of American grain, in Mark Lane! Can Mr Atkinson explain this failure of wheat and other food areas to expand, under the stimulus of his magical dollar a bushel in Mark Lane, during the first four years of the period covered by the table?

It appears that between 1889 and 1895 the wheat, rye, and buckwheat areas shrank 4,700,000 acres, as against an increase of 4,600,000 acres in the areas devoted to maize, oats, and potatoes, there being a decrease of 100,000 acres in the total area.

Since 1895, with maize and its secondary products, as well as oats, barley, rye, buckwheat, and potatoes bringing exceedingly low prices, the areas under those products have shrunk some 7,700,000 acres, while the area under wheat has increased by such reductions some 7,700,000 acres, with another 2,400,000 acres added from other sources, probably from reductions of the area under flax, hay, etc.

These reductions, or these conversions of something more tangible than a deficit (mostly in 1898) especially those of maize lands, seem to have been inevitable after an enormous substitution of cotton-seed oil for lard had reduced the herds of swine in the United States from 52,400,000 animals in 1892 to 39,800,000 animals in 1898, thus destroying the demand for hundreds of millions of bushels of maize. It seems not un-likely that similar reductions in the maize and oat fields of the United States will continue until the output of those grains has fallen below domestic requirements, when prices are likely to rise and cause another swing of the crop distribution pendulum.

Official United States reports, as late as January 1899, show a material increase of autumn wheat seeding, an indication of a continued reduction of the maize fields. From the foregoing it would appear that if any delusion exists in relation to this subject it does not rest with those who have foreseen such reductions.

Mr Atkinson tells us if we can only guarantee a dollar a bushel for wheat in Mark Lane, a hypothetical 64,000,000 acres of 15-bushel-an-acre land, for which he stands sponsor, will come im-immediately and permanently into cultivation. It seems, however, that the owners of some 10,000,000 acres of maize, hay, and oats lands did not require quite so decided a stimulant to prompt them to reduce the unprofitable acreages, and to increase the acreage of wheat. Is not this strange if the owners of 15-bushel-an-acre land are waiting especially for the price of 33s. a quarter in Mark Lane? It seems that owners of the 12-bushel-an-acre land are willing to change from maize and hay to wheat, and leave Mr Atkinson's 64,000,000 acres still idle!

The statement in my Address concerning the practically complete absorption of prairie lands adapted to wheat-growing, was based upon the fact that not only has settlement ceased to extend westward over prairies lying east of the Rocky Mountains, but, despite a vast increase in the number of would-be farmers, has been receding for more than ten years; indeed, the entire western border of the prairie region has been losing population, with a consequent abandonment of cultivation, in whole or in part, over immense areas. In 1893, when several millions of acres open to settlement were added to the lands of Oklahoma, there were ten applicants for every 160-acre tract available. Among these land-seekers were numbers who had crossed the continent westward in search of a home upon the public domain; but these nomads, not finding a desirable location on the Pacific slope, had returned nearly 2000 miles to seek an abiding-place in Oklahoma.

From the Canadian boundary, through the Dakotas, Nebraska, Eastern Colorado, Kansas, and Texas, the settlers in the early eighties marched up the great continental slope, in many cases beguiled by false representations as to the character of climate and soil. After exhausting their slender means, suffering repeated crop failures and desperate privations, these settlers were actually starved out, and compelled to return down the slope. The tide began to ebb in 1887, was at full flood from 1888 to 1894, and has not yet entirely ceased to flow. It is to be regretted that more is not known respecting this noiseless retreat of a great industrial army; but the biennial reports of the Kansas State Board of Agriculture and other official publications show that thirty-seven counties in the western third of that State lost 45 per cent. of population (an exclusively agricultural one) between 1888 and 1898. So great has been the dispersion that some of the counties retain barely sufficient people to conduct municipal and judicial affairs.

Farms and homes on the arid prairies were abandoned, not because of the unwillingness of the people to grow wheat at current prices, but because wheat refused to grow one year in three. The settlers exhausted their own means, and often that

of friends, and mortgaged their lands for the means
of subsistence.   Crops again failing, the unfortunates
were glad to accept loans of seed wheat from the
State and from railway companies, who made such
loans to retain population and traffic.   Despite these
efforts railways have been abandoned, and the rails
themselves removed from numbers of the luckless
districts.

Many of these facts are set forth in State publications ; likewise in reports of railway companies
with head offices in Boston, whose lines traverse
the arid regions of the Dakotas, Nebraska, Colorado,
Kansas,   Oklahoma,   and   Texas.   These   facts
should be familiar to Mr Atkinson, whose neigh-
bours in Boston, Brooklyn, and other Massachusetts
towns, made mortgage loans of vast sums in the
aggregate upon the lands of the arid plains which
since have been abandoned.   The mortgages have
been foreclosed, and the lenders still hold thousands
on thousands of acres of the drought-stricken lands
which never were fit for arable purposes, and from
which settlers have fled.

ARE THERE, AS ALLEGED, 64,000,000 ACRES OF UN-
    EMPLOYED WHEAT LANDS IN THE UNITED
    STATES FULLY SUITED TO THE PRODUCTION OF
    WHEAT AT 15 BUSHELS AN ACRE ?

In the most positive terms Mr Atkinson makes the statement that :—

"There are (in the United States) now fully 100,000 square miles of land, 64,000,000 acres, fully suitable to the production of wheat at 15 bushels to the acre, practically unoccupied in any branch of agriculture, which would be devoted to wheat on an assured price of a dollar a bushel (33s. a quarter) in Mark Lane, yielding 960,000,000 bushels."

This statement astonishes by its broad and absolute asseverations and by its manifold implications. It can be dissolved by one solitary fact.

Not a single State west and south from New York and east of the Rocky Mountains ever gave yields averaging 15 bushels an acre for even so short a term as five years. Of the 39,500,000 acres of wheat produced in the United States in 1897 quite five-sixths were grown east of the Rockies, and of this great aggregate New York and all New England contributed but 350,000 acres—less than 1 per cent.

It is interesting to contrast Mr Atkinson's statement with a paragraph from a recent paper by Mr John Hyde, Statistician of the U.S. Department of Agriculture, who says : " That for general agricultural purposes the public domain is practically exhausted, and that consequently there can be no

E

further considerable addition to the farm area of the country, is too well established a fact to be the subject of controversy."

INDIAN TERRITORY.

Mr Atkinson asks :—

"If John Bull, in place of building granaries, could offer 33s. a quarter, or a dollar a bushel, in London, as a permanent price for the next thirty years, would not Uncle Sam accept the offer? And if Uncle Sam should then ask for bids among the States, are there not several single States or Territories that would take the contract each for itself?"

"Having put that question I now propose to submit an enquiry in due form in order to sustain my own belief that we can supply the whole present and the increasing demand of Great Britain for the next thirty years with 6 bushels of wheat per head, at a dollar a bushel, from land situated wholly in the Indian territory, not yet open to private entry, but which may soon be open when the Indian titles have all been purchased."

This comprehensive statement is staggering to the average Briton, who naturally will be tempted to enquire how *a present demand* for 240,000,000 bushels of wheat can be met from lands not yet open to settlement, and consequently not prepared for wheat production!

It is officially stated, in the latest issue of the

" Statistical Abstract of the United States," that the Indian Territory has an area of 31,000 square miles of land surface, of which almost every acre is in the communal possession of various tribes of Indians. Treaties for the segregation of the Cherokee and Creek lands have already been made, and the other tribes will doubtless follow shortly. These treaties provide that all the lands shall be equally distributed among the members of each tribe, thus shutting out the white man, except as the tenant of an Indian landlord, and the lands being unalienable for about a generation, it is difficult to see how an annual 240,000,000 bushels of wheat can be exported from this source just at present ! That some of the lands of the Indian Territory are as fertile as those of adjoining districts in Kansas, Oklahoma, Arkansas, and Texas is unquestioned, but they are not all fertile—far from it. Moreover, the Texan district, immediately south of the Territory that lies east of the 95th meridian, is ill adapted to wheat growing ; the same may be said of that eastward in Arkansas, while south-eastern Kansas is but a moderately fair wheat region. In fact, the whole eastern third of Kansas in 1895 grew but 500,000 acres out of a State total of 5,150,000 acres. Eastern Kansas is a maize and cattle country, and the eastern part or possibly the whole of the Indian Territory is better adapted to maize and cattle than to wheat.

The eastern half of the prolongation of the "Flint Hills" of Kansas invades the Territory, and along the Verdigris River and its tributaries the valleys are mostly narrow, and the uplands rocky and sterile, and certainly not adapted to wheat growing. The same may be said of the spurs of the Ozarks which project into the Territory from Missouri and Arkansas, on its eastern border. Of less than 20,000,000 acres included in the Indian country it is safe to say not more than one-half will be brought into cultivation within the next thirty years—if, indeed, so much as half is cultivable.

Probably nowhere in the world, outside the maritime plain of Eastern China, are there *vast tracts* of land where so large a proportion of the surface is adapted to cultivation as in the great States of Illinois and Iowa, where the lands are more fully employed than in · any equal area in either America or Europe. Yet neither of these rich States has 55 per cent. of its surface under harvested staples, including hay. The proportion of tillable land in the eastern two-thirds of Kansas is as great as in the Indian Territory, and yet of this area, cultivated by whites, hardly 44 per cent. bears harvested crops, including the unbroken prairie mown for hay. It is possible that in thirty years the Indian titles will have been extinguished, railways built, and 44 per cent. of the Indian lands brought under culture, although this with a mixed population would equal the progress made in forty-four years in Kansas.

Keeping in view the fact that there are less than 20,000,000 acres of good, bad, and indifferent lands, that even at an average of fifteen bushels an acre, it will require 16,000,000 acres to meet *present* British requirements for wheat, the lands being still in possession of Indians, it may be pertinent to ask how is it possible to supply even a tenth part of present British requirements. How long must Britain wait to secure the promised supply upon the assumption that it must all come from less than 12,000,000 cultivable acres, provided the required 33s. were guaranteed? Has not Mr Atkinson tripped in his calculation, when he proposes to meet the requirements of each of the next thirty years from lands not yet open to settlement, and that may not be open till half or three-fourths the term has expired?

OKLAHOMA.

It is doubtless true there are areas of uncultivated prairie in Oklahoma as well as in the

Indian Territory from which Oklahoma was detached, but these areas are neither unoccupied nor unemployed. Such portions of Oklahoma as are not occupied by outsiders are still in the possession of Indian tribes, whose members own herds of cattle grazing upon tribal lands, while other tribal lands have been rented to white graziers, and contribute to the meat supply of Europe and of America. In time, more or less remote, parts of these lands will be allotted to the members of the tribes, and the remainder to scrambling whites.

Practically, all that part of Oklahoma lying west of a line extending from the 98th meridian on its northern border to the 100th meridian on its southern boundary, is unfit for cereal culture, because of aridity. Cultivable Oklahoma comprises but some 12,000 square miles, of which less than 6,000,000 acres are really worth cultivation. There are large tracts of sandy " black-jack " land, the very name indicating that it will grow little else than the " black-jack " oak, a synonym of sterility, while along the Caney river and its tributaries much of the surface is so rough and rocky as to be adapted only to grazing, while the narrow valleys are subject to overflow. This rocky hill region is but a prolongation of the sterile " Flint Hills " of Kansas.

Notwithstanding these facts, Mr Atkinson asks Englishmen to believe that if a dollar a bushel is offered for wheat in Mark Lane, the least extensive of western wheat-growing districts will at once add 3,200,000 acres to its productive area, when its entire cultivable portion, likely to remain for a greater or less number of years in the communal possession of Indian tribes, does not exceed 6,000,000 acres, nearly all of which are now employed in growing harvested crops, or in grazing cattle just as essential as crops, and quite as profitable as wheat at a dollar a bushel in Mark Lane. More and more of the lands of Oklahoma are devoted to cotton, and give nearly if not quite the highest yields known in the United States.

Mr Atkinson asserts that Oklahoma, although only opened to settlement seven years ago, will this year produce 13,000,000 bushels of wheat. He does not tell us in how many of the seven years the crops have failed, nor in how many the settler, because of such failure, has been forced to borrow seed wheat on the condition that the lender shall have a third or half of the produce when thrashed; nor does he tell us how often the rich, narrow valleys of Eastern Oklahoma overflow. An important statement of this economist is in direct

conflict with the public records of the United States,
which show that the lands of Oklahoma were opened
to settlement in April, 1889, instead of 1891, as
would follow if opened only seven years prior to
October, 1898, and that the territory was organised
on the 2nd of May, 1890, a year earlier than Mr
Atkinson places the opening of the lands. Nor
does Mr Atkinson point out that both settlement
and population are conditions precedent to the
organisation of a territorial government; and he
fails to note that the census taken in June, 1890,
shows Oklahoma as having 61,834 inhabitants
besides Indians, and some 50,000 acres under
᾽ ᾽rvested crops, including hay. These economic
e. rors and omissions would be immaterial, except
that they show the rapidity with which prairie lands
are brought into production. As a matter of fact,
Greer County, Oklahoma, so long claimed by
Texas, was settled even long before 1889.

TEXAS.

Here is another specimen of Mr Atkinson's
illusions :—

" I undertake to say that the State of Texas can meet
this whole demand without impairing in the slightest
degree its present products of grain, cotton, wool, and

meats, and without appropriating the use of more than a small fraction of the area of that single State, which has not yet been fenced in or subjected to the plough to the production of wheat."

This statement is more remarkable for omissions than for positive averments. The land surface of Texas has an area of 167,866,000 acres, and no intimation being given that all this vast area is not "fully suitable to the production of wheat at fifteen bushels to the acre," it follows that such inference may fairly be drawn. Mr Atkinson omits to inform his readers that only one-sixth of the area of Texas —included between the 96th meridian on the east, the 100th meridian on the west, the Red River the north, and latitude 30° 30' on the south, or .n *enclave* facing Red River of barely 28,000,000 acres —is by soil and climate, adapted to successful wheat culture. Of the sixty counties constituting the wheat district of Texas, twelve in the southern corners of the *enclave* are not well adapted to wheat ; and outside this comparatively limited section profitable wheat-growing is impracticable, except upon a few thousand acres of irrigated lands, and other small areas susceptible of irrigation. He could easily have added that in all that portion of the State lying west of the 100th meridian—some 77,000,000 acres—cereal culture, except on irrigated

lands, is precluded by an arid climate ; that nowhere
in the United States does the wheat plant thrive
south of latitude 30° ; that nearly or quite
40,000,000 acres of Texan lands lie below the 30th
parallel, and that wheat does not thrive in the
humid atmosphere and amid the cypress swamps,
common to that great fraction of Texas lying east
of the 95th meridian west of Greenwich.

Mr Atkinson also might have told us that when
the federal census was taken in 1890, the one-sixth
of the area of Texas included in the *enclave* of sixty
counties already cited produced 96 per cent. of the
wheat grown in the State ; no less than 57 per cent.
of the cotton ; 51 per cent. of cereals of every
description, and a large proportion of both horses
and cattle.   And he might have added that this
fraction of one-sixth constitutes the very heart and
body of agricultural Texas ; that its sixty counties
of less than average size, are by all odds the most
prosperous, productive, and progressive of the 203,
and that since the census year greater development,
both agricultural and commercial, as well as
industrial, has there obtained than in any or all of
the other 143 counties.   Mr Atkinson would have
been fully warranted had he added that from either
an agricultural or economic standpoint the sixty
counties of the only potential wheat district in the

State, as herein outlined, are worth twice as much as all the vast remainder of Texas.

Mr Atkinson also should tell us how much of Texas is fenced, how much ploughed, and how at the average rate of yield of Texan wheat-fields (10.5 bushels an acre) it would require 22,600,000 acres to supply his promised 240,000,000 bushels of wheat. We should then be in possession of facts sufficient to determine how the sixty counties would appear, in the height of the growing season, with their fields yielding some 8,000,000 acres of cotton, maize, oats and other grains, and with an added 22,600,000 acres of wheat, all emplaced on a total of 28,000,000 acres of rock-bound hills, sterile sandy ridges, chapparal covered mountains, and fertile prairies. If these omissions were supplied, we should know what credit to accord Mr Atkinson's statement that Texas can furnish 240,000,000 bushels of wheat annually, in addition to that required for home consumption.

To show how completely Mr Atkinson's hasty assertions differ from those of Mr Hyde, the statistician already referred to, I will quote this latter gentleman's views on the possibilities of Oklahoma and Texas :—

" In Tennessee, Texas, and Oklahoma the conditions are somewhat different from those obtaining in the other

States south of the 37th parallel, but the favourable conditions that render possible the larger production in these
States are more or less localised, and no really great extension of this branch of agriculture is to be looked for
within their borders, even under the stimulus of higher
prices."

SOUTHERN STATES.

After assigning to Texas the task of supplying
the entire wheat needs of the British Isles, Mr
Atkinson says :—

"To satisfy the anxieties of Sir William Crookes, lest
land should be taken from other necessary work, this area
might be divided among several States and territories, say
5000 square miles (each) among eight."

His selected regions comprise Oklahoma, the
Virginia Valley of the Shenandoah and its
tributaries, Kentucky, Tennessee, Kansas, Nebraska,
Minnesota, and the two Dakotas ; the last five he
remarks "would compete for the contract, to each
open a little patch of 5000 square miles, *not yet
adjacent to railways.*"

As to the Valley of the Shenandoah—better
known until "Sheridan's ride" as the "Valley of
Virginia"—we find the addition of 3,200,000 cultivated acres in this limited area a puzzle, as some
2,500,000 possibly cultivable acres were occupied

and tilled since early in the eighteenth century, when the hardy Scots migrated to the " Valley " in the track of the first white man (Governor Spotswood) who first visited that delightful region in 1716. The cultivable portion of this entire region is limited practically to that part of the valley, 160 miles long by an average of 20 in width, lying between Harper's Ferry on the Potomac and the town of Lexington at the south. South of Lexington the lands are so broken that the region is not adapted to agricultural operations on any considerable scale. The lands of the " Valley " proper are exceedingly fertile, abounding in fields, meadows, orchards, and farmyards, and leave little room for Mr Atkinson's proposed 3,200,000 additional acres.

The impracticable character of the task assigned to this limited Virginian district becomes apparent when we learn from the reports of the U.S. Department of Agriculture, that although Virginia was settled about 300 years ago, yet in 1897 the entire State had less than 3,800,000 acres under such crops as grain, hay, cotton, tobacco, and potatoes, and that in no year have such crops covered as many as 4,500,000 acres. Nor must we lose sight of the fact that the " Valley " comprises but a small part of Virginia's 25,000,000

acres, and that a local price for wheat equal to
the minimum which Mr Atkinson indicates as
highly stimulative of production has not served
to increase the acres devoted to that crop; wheat
now covers barely a fifth as many acres as he
proposes to add in a remote corner of the State,
and the harvests of the ten years ending with
1896 gave yields averaging a slender 6·9 bushels
an acre, while the State's wheat crops, exclusive
of the seed required, have aggregated little more
than 5,000,000 bushels per annum.

Kentucky's cultivable lands are as completely
occupied as those of Virginia, and the promise
for an expansion of the wheat-fields is no greater,
although the yields average two bushels more
an acre.

Eastern Tennessee offers considerable areas
that in time may be devoted to wheat, but the
prospect is not such as to excite hope of increasing
the State's low average yield of 8·4 bushels an
acre. Adding 3,200,000 acres to the cultivable
land of Tennessee, probably an impracticable task,
would not materially add to the supply of wheat,
if, as indicated by Mr Atkinson, wheat only
occupied one-fourth the added acres in a four
course rotation, since the yield, exclusive of seed,
is less than seven bushels an acre, and the added

wheat area would give crops (net) of not more than 6,000,000 bushels per annum.

Virginia, Kentucky, and Tennessee are long settled, and their lands, where not sterile, are fully occupied, but their meagre yields testify to weak productive power.

If, as Mr Atkinson states, "the partially exhausted soils of the South" are in course of rapid renovation by the use of legumes, this amendment is not reflected in the crop reports, which show no increase of acre-yields even for short terms of years. This failure of the legume treatment indicates the seeming necessity of a long course of the restorative "cow peas" and "gruber nuts," in order to bring the low southern average of 7·8 bushels of wheat an acre even up to the 12·7 bushels average of the United States, and a still longer course to raise the average to the boasted fifteen bushels.

Obviously, not many of the 64,000,000 acres, vaunted as "fully suitable to the production of wheat at fifteen bushels to the acre and practically unoccupied in any branch of agriculture," are to be found in the South.

Mr Atkinson's calculations make no provision whatever for seed. Estimates are formulated as though all the wheat harvested was available for food! Yields of wheat as low as the southern average of 7·8 bushels indicate the absorption of at least one-fifth (20 per cent.) in seeding the fields.

THE GREAT WHEAT STATES.

Referring to Mr Atkinson's statement that

"Kansas, Nebraska, Minnesota, and the two Dakotas would compete for the contract each to open a little patch of 5000 square miles not yet adjacent to railways,"

it appears sufficient to say that no evidence is forthcoming as to the existence of a single patch of 5000 square miles of cultivable land not adjacent to some railway. Certainly there is no such "patch" in Nebraska or in Kansas. In fact, in neither of these two States is there a cultivable "patch" of even 500 square miles that is not within fifteen miles of a railway, and the western farmer rarely or never complains if he can market wheat by carting it fifteen miles. A glance at the map of Kansas shows there is no part of the eastern and cultivable two-thirds of the State, except in the barren "Flint Hills," so far away as fifteen miles from a railway. Railway facilities are little less favourable even in the more recently settled Dakotas, and railway companies compete

sharply for the privilege of furnishing any productive region with new lines.

Tables giving the nutritive equivalent of other
grains, and potential energy of given weights
thereof, are furnished by Mr Atkinson, who considers other grains, and the toothsome " Boston
baked bean" foods as desirable as wheat. But the
question is not of baked beans, nor of maize, nor
of the substitution of any other food product for
wheat ; nor is it a question as to the sufficiency or
credibility of the opinions of Presidents of the
various Produce Exchanges, or of the learned men
who conduct experiments at the Agricultural Stations
provided in the Hatch enactment. It is simply, as
stated in my Address before the British Association,
a question whether each unit of designated populations shall in future be able to command the
accustomed (average) annual ration of wheat, or
one equalling 4.5 bushels for each unit of such
population—a given proportion of such ration being
used as food and the remainder as seed.

The problem so stated by me and so limited,
involves the future of the United States as wheat
grower, consumer, and exporter.

Mr Atkinson shows the relation of cultivated
areas in the United States to the total area, but does
he show the real relations between the acres already

F

in production to the *cultivable* portion of the whole
area as clearly as is possible or desirable in a discussion of this nature? Neither has he directed
attention to the futility of attempting to show
the productive power of any region by so simple
and easy a process as comparing the lands employed
in actual production with the entire number of acres
—good, bad, and indifferent—included in the whole.
Let me endeavour to arrive at a correct understand-
ing of the United States agricultural potentiality by
being explicit where he is vague.

Accepting official American determinations, we
find that Colorado, Wyoming, Montana, Idaho,
Nevada, Utah, Arizona, and New Mexico have
areas aggregating some 556,000,000 acres, or about
870,000 square miles. This vast region is made up
of plains, mountains, and basin plateaus so arid as
to be of infinitesimal value for food production
relatively to the whole area—except such food as
results from pastoral pursuits. That is to say, the
agricultural value of this vast area is on a par with
that of the least productive equal area in Central
Asia. Outside a very few small districts like Latah
county, Idaho, cereal culture without irrigation is
impossible. This is evident from the fact that the
comparatively large mining population is still dependent for much of its food upon the lowland

humid regions, notwithstanding the fact that these mining districts in many cases have been longer settled than the adjacent humid areas. This is made still clearer by the following statement, which shows the area producing cultivated staples in all the eight States and Territories as late as 1897.

TABLE XIII.

Area under Grains and Hay in Mountain States and Territories in 1897.

	Acres
Wheat	810,000
All other grains . . .	477,000
Hay	1,926,000
Total acres under staples .	3,213,000

This area, contributory to the food supply of the mountain population, nominally is six-tenths of 1 per cent. of the whole, but really is but three-tenths of 1 per cent., as most of the hay is consumed by draught animals employed in mining, and in commercial operations directly related to mining. In the mountain districts vegetables and fruits are grown for local consumption on irrigated lands, and small quantities are exported to the humid districts.

The eight States and Territories specifically named cover but 70 per cent. of the arid region, which includes bordering tracts in Texas, Oklahoma,

Kansas, Nebraska, the Dakotas, California, Oregon, and Washington, aggregating an additional area of 180,000,000 acres or more, the whole barren region comprising some 736,000,000 acres. Over this vast region, with insignificant exceptions similar to the Latah district in Idaho, cereal culture is impracticable without irrigation.

When the census was taken in 1890, the eight mountain States and Territories contained 2,300,000 irrigated acres, although parts of this region had been settled and irrigation practised by the Spaniards two centuries before the Mormons made the utmost of the narrow valleys of Utah. The difficulty is the absence of available water to irrigate more than 2 or at most 3 per cent. of this stupendous region. Similar conditions existing in that portion of the arid belt not included in the eight States and Territories, the course of production will there be much the same, although with a smaller mining population possibly a larger proportion of the irrigated plots could be devoted to cereals.

In an attempt to gauge even approximately the power of the United States to grow cereals, the entire 736,000,000 acres or more of the arid belt must be rigidly excluded from the equation : it is none the less necessary to exclude at least nine-tenths of all the region south of the Virginias,

North Carolina, Kentucky, and Tennessee east of the Mississippi, the half of Arkansas, all of Louisiana, and that portion of Texas lying east of the 100th meridian and south of latitude 30, or an additional 210,000,000 acres. That this great tract is practically worthless for cereal production, other than maize, is evident from the fact that in 1897 it grew less than 350,000 acres of wheat, and only 1,200,000 acres of oats. The employment of so small a proportion of the whole area in grain growing, other than maize, is due to the paucity of the yields per acre, which average less than 7 bushels of wheat, as against 14 in most northern wheat-growing districts, 14 bushels of maize as against 28 bushels in the ten greatest producing States, and less than half as many bushels of oats an acre as are grown in the United States as a whole. In fact, the potential of the cotton belt for cereals is so low that it requires 2,500,000 acres to grow as much wheat, exclusive of that used for seed, as is grown upon 1,000,000 acres north of the Potomac and Ohio rivers. Neither the soil nor the climate of the cotton-growing region is adapted to the production of profitable crops of wheat, rye, barley, or oats, therefore that entire region should be excluded from the equation in estimating the power of the United States to grow the bread required by populations of Caucasian race. In other words, the real potential is that of the 947,000,000 acres that remain after eliminating the arid districts and the more southerly portion of the cotton region. Of this 947,000,000 acres, some 217,000,000 are employed as follows :—

TABLE XIV.

	Acres.
Maize	77,700,000
Wheat	44,000,000
Oats	25,800,000
Barley	2,600,000
Rye	1,600,000
Buckwheat . . .	700,000
Potatoes . . .	2,600,000
Tobacco	600,000
Hay	42,800,000
Flax and Hemp . . .	1,500,000
Pulse	1,500,000
Market gardens, etc. . .	4,000,000
Truck farms . . .	700,000
Vineyards . . .	800,000
Nurseries and seed farms .	500,000
Hops and broom-corn . .	200,000
Sorghum	800,000
Dhouras	500,000
Small fruits . . .	500,000
Farm gardens . . .	2,000,000
Orchards (nuts and fruits) .	4,500,000
Lucerne	800,000
Sweet potatoes . . .	300,000
TOTAL . . .	217,000,000

On farms situated on what may be termed the cultivable or cereal half of the United States there are some 54,000,000 horses, mules, and cattle ; each animal requires about 3 acres of the sandy, brushy, hilly, broken, and swampy lands constituting average pasture, thus absorbing some 162,000,000 acres ; while roads, railways, parks, cemeteries, villages, towns, and other public developments occupy at least 50,000,000 other acres, and the lands wholly waste, or covered with forest growths, and not cultivable, or even available for pasture, constitute at least 80 per cent. of the entire remainder. This leaves something like 100,000,000 acres, of which possibly one half may be productive within thirty years ; but even then it will be largely devoted to grazing and to the production of hay needed by the draught and dairy animals required to serve a rapidly increasing population. Possibly 25 of the 100,000,000 acres may be devoted to harvested crops other than hay ; but the present population requiring that nearly ninety animals shall be kept on the farms for every hundred people (wholly exclusive of the number kept in towns), there must be forage and pasturage for at least 1,250,000 animals for each year's addition to the population, and this necessitates at least 4 acres for pasturage and hay for each animal so added, a demand that would absorb the entire available 100,000,000 acres in twenty years—unless the standard of living be reduced.

It appears that little, if any, of the scattered fragments of the cultivable area of the United States can be relied on to contribute to the bread supply of the world, although, as stated in my Address, it is possible to increase the supply by scientific fertilisation. Artificial stimulation would involve large expenditure per acre for nitrogenous and other manures, an outlay which the cultivator will be slow to incur until higher prices warrant the outlay. Neither fertilisation nor rotation is practised in the great American wheat districts to any considerable extent; their general use will imply higher prices, and higher prices imply comparative scarcity.

Mr Atkinson is credited with the statement that annual unit consumption of wheat in the United States was at the rate of the equivalent of a barrel of flour, or 4.5 bushels, or 0.4 (four-tenths) the average net yield of an acre, exclusive of that required for seed. The present population, estimated by the Treasury Department at 74,500,000, would therefore require the average net product from 29,800,000 acres out of some 44,100,000 estimated to have been harvested in 1898, leaving for export the product of 14,300,000 acres when yields are average.

As it is easy to determine the requirements for the other staples, it does not seem difficult to foretell the date when the United States will probably cease to export food.

The area employed in oats during the seven years ending with 1897 having averaged 27,200,000 acres per annum, and the exports averaging 20,900,000 bushels per annum, or the net product from 901,000 acres per annum, and the mean population for the seven years amounting to 68,300,000, it follows that each average unit of the population required and consumed the net product of 0.38 of an acre of oats. Pursuing a like calculation with each of the products, it is found that *for purely domestic consumption* the average unit's area quota under all harvested products other than cotton has been 2.884 acres, divided as follows :—

TABLE XV.

	Unit's Area Quota.
Maize	1.000
Wheat.	0.402
Oats	0.380
Rye, barley, buckwheat, and potatoes	0.122
Hay	0.685
Tobacco, flax, and hemp . .	0.031
Orchards, gardens, and minor crops .	0.264
TOTAL . . .	2.884 acres

If it is a fact that the average unit of the population requires 2.884 acres under the products named
for purely domestic consumption, and at least 2
acres in pasturage for proportion of horses and
cattle, then it requires the addition annually of
some 7,000,000 acres to meet each year's added
needs. At this rate the possible 100,000,000 acres of
available lands, and the 25,000,000 now employed
for growing grains for export in primary and
secondary forms will be absorbed by the addition
of 26,000,000 people, and at the present rate of
increase this multitude will be added in less than
twenty years. Thus, a quarter of a century hence,
exports will only be possible either from an increase
of acre yields, or from a material lowering of the
standard of living, or from both combined.

Mr Atkinson's rash statements do not corre-
spond with the hard facts of the case, and should
be accepted with caution.

Passing to secondary criticisms, I select a few
of the most prominent, to show that many who
differ from the statements in my Address have
but imperfectly mastered its contents.

ENGLISH *versus* AMERICAN FARMING.

In the same critique Sir John Lawes and Sir
Henry Gilbert are unjust to the great mass of

American farmers in attributing meagre yields of wheat from American fields to poor husbandry. They say that—

"In the case of the growth of an average of more than 13 bushels per acre for fifty years in succession without manure at Rothamsted, the land has been kept as free from weeds as is possible. On the other hand, most of the export lands of the United States are scarcely more than skimmed by the plough, scarcely any labour is bestowed on cleaning ; weeds largely rob the fertility ; the straw and weeds are to a great extent burnt, and manure is often wasted. . . . It is impossible to believe that the wheat-growing acres of the United States, which are said to be already showing exhaustion, would not, with good cultivation, yield large crops for many years yet . . . but failure to utilise the existing fertility is the cause of the restricted yield."

In the above passage the writers appear to base their conclusions upon "it is said" rather than on official data readily available in the Reports of the Federal Department of Agriculture. These show the increased yield from an average of 12 bushels an acre in the eleven years ending 1890, to 12.7 bushels an acre for the ten years ending 1896. An increase of nearly 6 per cent. certainly affords no basis for the inference of exhaustion.

It is true that straw is sometimes burnt in the newer districts, and some manure may be wasted, yet such practices are rare, and do not occur over enough of the wheat area to appreciably affect production. The "restricted yields" are not due to any lack of fertility, or failure to utilise it, but almost entirely to climatic conditions, which limit American yields as they so largely do those of England. American farmers are no more disposed than are those of Great Britain or their sons in the Canadian North-West, to "scarcely more than skim by the plough." Where this is done, barring exceptional cases, it is because climatic conditions prevent better work. For instance, the Official Handbook of the Dominion, issued in 1896, states that in 1895, the ground freezing before the completion of the harvest in Manitoba, farmers were unable to plough their fields for seeding in 1896, and the spring of 1896 being of a character to prevent the completion of this work, wheat was sown on the unploughed stubble, and the yield thereby was greatly reduced, as well as the area. In Kansas, and other States, the farmers are often forced to wait one, two, and even three months for rains that will enable them to plough the baked fields ; poor yields result because of late preparation ; and they are charged with neglecting cultivation by critics 5000 miles off, knowing nothing of the environing conditions! American methods are quite as well adapted to the soils and climate as are those of England to the soils and climate of Great Britain.

By at least one English authority France is designated as the best cultivated country in Europe, yet the maize fields of France give yields averaging less than 18 bushels an acre, those of Italy and Roumania but 15 bushels, and those of Russia but 12 bushels, while those of Austria-Hungary, with cultivation certainly much inferior to that of France, give yields of 21 bushels. In the United States, maize averages over 23 imperial bushels an acre, rising to 28 bushels in the seven great maize-growing States ! The fact is, that American farming is not so very defective; that meagre yields of wheat are no more indicative of poor farming than are yields of maize in France below those of the great maize belt of America; nor are great English yields of wheat (still a fourth less than those of Hesse and Denmark) even presumptive evidence that English methods are better adapted to British conditions than are those of the United States to American conditions of climate and soil.

Are not greater yields of maize than elsewhere quite as good proof of the superiority of American methods as are yields of wheat in England that are exceeded elsewhere? In each case the result is due very much more largely, if not wholly, to atmospheric than cultural conditions, and special adaptation to certain staples. Methods have simply been conformed to the environment.

That it is possible for Sir John Lawes and Sir Henry Gilbert to overlook well-established facts would appear from their statement that—

" The truth is that we (in Great Britain) produce more per acre of every staple food suited to our soil and climate than any other country in the world. But we have a greater population in proportion to our cultivable area than any other country in Europe."

I do not know what staple foods these authorities had in their minds when making this assertion, but if they meant it to be understood that Great Britain grew greater yields per acre of wheat, barley, oats, and potatoes than those grown anywhere in the world, the statement is incorrect. As regards wheat, Denmark has grown crops of wheat averaging 40 bushels an acre since 1883, as against an average of about 29.5 bushels in the United Kingdom ; Hesse, also, when an independent State, grew greater acre yields of wheat than Britain, and this is even now true, although it is obscured by the remainder of Germany. Holland has grown crops of barley and oats, respectively, giving average yields of 40 and 43 bushels an acre, as compared with yields averaging but 33 and 38 bushels an acre in the British Isles; whilst in respect to potatoes, Great Britain is surpassed by Belgium. In making the statement that the United Kingdom has a greater population in proportion to cultivable area than any country in Europe, Sir John Lawes and Sir Henry Gilbert seem to have forgotten Switzerland.

In attributing the cessation of the bringing into production of new wheat-bearing acres in the United States, as well as in other countries, to falls in price since about 1885, Sir John Lawes and Sir Henry Gilbert offer no explanation of a continued increase of maize and oats areas, despite falls in prices for those grains. The wheat area ceased to expand in the United States not because of a fall in price, but because farmers found it necessary to provide large quantities of hay, maize, and oats for great additions to their herds of domestic animals. That that price was not even a minor factor has been made plain by the avidity with which settlers seized upon every fraction of an Indian reservation opened to settlement. When the lands of Oklahoma were thrown open to settlement, there were twenty claimants for every tract the size of an average farm.

WHEAT AND MEAN TEMPERATURE

In December last, in their letter to *The Times*, Sir John Lawes and Sir Henry Gilbert misunderstood my views about the food supply of the United Kingdom. I said that in case of an European war wheat would certainly be declared contraband. I spoke on the one hand of national granaries, and on the other of growing the whole of our own requirements ourselves. In either case the outlay would be vast, and I did not venture to decide which would be most practicable. To quote my own words—I said : "We eagerly spend millions to protect our coasts and commerce, and millions more on ships, explosives, guns, and men, but we omit to take necessary precautions to supply ourselves with the very first and supremely important munition of war—food." Doubt is thrown on my statement that almost yearly, since 1885, additions to the wheat-growing area of the United States have diminished. The following figures, taken from official sources, illustrate my meaning. I have condensed them into five-yearly averages, omitting smaller figures. In 1883-87 the annual average under wheat in the United States was 37,000,000 acres, in 1888-92 38,000,000 acres, and in 1893-97 35,500,000. Thus, the whole wheat acreage in the

United States is less than fifteen years ago, and of the 8,000,000 acres added to the world's wheat since 1882 not one is contributed by the United States.

Commenting on my statement that "the ripening of wheat requires a temperature averaging at least 65° for 55 to 65 days," Sir J. Lawes and Sir H. Gilbert declare this rule does not apply to Great Britain, as heavy English crops were grown in 1854, when the average for July and August was only just over 61°. Their error arises from the quotation of a sentence apart from the context. Let me supply the omission. My sentence runs : " Considering Siberia as a wheat-grower, climate is the first consideration. Summers are short—as they are in all regions with Continental climates north of the 45th parallel—and the ripening of wheat requires a temperature averaging at least 65° F. for 55 to 65 days." It is plain I was dealing with Siberian conditions. It is well known that wheat, in a soft, humid, equable climate, like that of England, Denmark, or New Zealand, will ripen with a mean temperature of 60° prolonged from 60 to 65 days ; yet so essential is the required temperature in the season of maturation, that in 1853 the yield of English wheat-fields was reduced about one-half owing to the mean for July and August falling to

G

57° to 59° in the wheat districts of England—a reduction of but 2° below *minimum* requirements for
those months.

As altitudes increase, or wherever the climate
assumes a Continental and variable character, mean
summer temperatures rising even to 68° are required over large areas, the mean for most interior
Continental regions being about 65°, as in Siberia
and the Canadian North-West.

When the night temperature sinks below a
certain point, growth and ripening cease for the
time being. Hence a higher mean temperature is
required in countries having a Continental climate,
and this mean must extend over a longer period
than in warmer and more equable climates, where
the ripening process is compressed within 55 days,
and the day and night temperatures do not differ
more than a fourth as much as do the day and night
temperatures of Siberia or the Canadian North-
West.

In Kansas, wheat ripens in from 27 to 30 days
from the time it blossoms; the exact time, with the
same variety of wheat, depending on the heat and
moisture. A high, moist temperature ripens it
prematurely, and gives a shrivelled grain, reducing
the yield one-half as it did with all the late wheat
in 1897, while wheat sown earlier ripened before the

coming of the humid heat, and gave full, plump, and bright grains, weighing twice as much per acre.

The climate of St Petersburg, although it may be termed maritime, and the district little above sea-level, is not adapted to wheat-growing, despite the fact that the mean summer temperature is 60.6°. Blodget in his "Climatology" says, at page 215 : "The vicinity of St Petersburg is known to be scarcely cultivable for any grains, and wholly un-profitable for wheat, and at Veliki-Oustoug, on the same parallel, and 15° of longitude eastward, is found the defined limits of all grains ; wheat not growing so far, and being uncultivable beyond the Volga."

In Central Russia wheat is not grown in any part where the summer heat has not a mean of 64°. It does not follow that wheat will not grow over restricted areas at temperatures somewhat lower than those named, but, as a rule, successful wheat culture demands arbitrary climatic conditions.

Canada's Position as an Exporter of Wheat.

General critics, especially those of the *Toronto Globe, Outlook,* and *Newcastle Journal,* have called

attention to what they deem a too limited measure-
ment of the power of Canada to produce wheat.
The *Toronto Globe* throws down the challenge in
the following fashion :—

" In 1895 Manitoba, with 25,000 farmers, grew
60,000,000 bushels of grain, about half of which was
wheat. Other grains were grown because the price for
wheat was so low as to leave little for the grower ; that
prices were so low the following season that a smaller area
was devoted to wheat ; that the area of the Province is
about 40,000,000 acres, of which much is lake surface, but
if we put the cultivatable portion at half the whole, what
will 20,000,000 acres produce if 1,000,000 grows 25,000,000
bushels? Manitoba is, however, but a fraction of the
Canadian North-West, and three or four Manitobas can be
carved out of the Westland. When that is exhausted,
there remains the Peace River district, where, it is asserted,
half the wheat supply of the world can be grown."

It is stated by the *Toronto Globe* that other
grains were grown in 1896, and not exclusively
wheat, because of the low price of wheat. If that
was the incentive prompting the growth of 637,000
acres of barley and oats, why were not the 1,140,000
acres employed in growing wheat devoted to the
more profitable grains? Why grow twice as much
wheat as the more remunerative staples ?

Referring to the *Toronto Globe's* statement that
the wheat area was reduced because of the low price

of wheat, it is not out of place to ask what cause
was in operation to reduce the barley and oats areas
by 10.5 per cent in 1896? It could hardly be the
low price of wheat. As the wheat area of North
Dakota, adjoining Manitoba on the south, shrunk
15 per cent. in 1896, and that decline is there attri-
buted to the unfavourable character of a season
that prevented the ploughing and seeding of many
fields, it is probable that the cause of the reduction
of all Manitobian grain areas in 1896 is correctly
stated on page 81 of the " Official Handbook of the
Dominion of Canada," published by the Dominion
Department of the Interior. In the "Handbook" it
is stated that the crop of 1895 was not fully harvested
until the ground froze, leaving no time for fall
ploughing; and the spring of 1896, because of
heavy rains, being unusually late, farmers were
forced to sow much of the wheat that was planted
on unploughed stubble. In view of conditions of
like character in Dakota, we may assume that the
Handbook hits on the true cause of the area
decline.

The *Toronto Globe's* statement, in relation to the
character of much of Manitoba's surface, is doubtless
correct as far as it goes, but it omits to tell that
much of the area, especially in the north-eastern
half of the province, is ill adapted to wheat, even

upon so much of the land surface as is cultivable. It also fails to note the significant fact that, while the entire south-western third of Manitoba is fairly gridironed with railways, there are no railways (but the main line into Winnipeg from the east) in all the north-eastern half, and that in America, railways are keen to occupy, before their rivals, even un-settled but potentially productive regions. Possibly the fact that the summer isotherm of 65° lies well south in Eastern Manitoba, and the fact that wheat on interior areas rarely ripens north of such line, has something to do with the abstention of railways to occupy the regions east of Lakes Manitoba and Winnipeg.

Apparently the *Toronto Globe* has not thought the matter of sufficient importance, or it would have informed its readers that as long ago as 1891 it was officially stated that no less than 63 per cent. of the cultivable lands of the public domain of Manitoba had been taken up by settlers. Nor does it make mention of the fact that the grain area of 1896 was but 60,000 acres greater than in 1893.

Doubtless in Assiniboia, and possibly in Sas-katchewan, there is much good wheat land, but the whole area is not adapted to wheat, neither is all the land cultivable. In the aggregate, there are large water surfaces, and other equally large surfaces utterly worthless except for grazing. The western half of Assiniboia, and probably a large proportion of Saskatchewan, is too parched for cereal culture except by irrigation, and it is not probable in such thirsty districts water can be obtained to irrigate more than 5 per cent. of the surface. West from Manitoba is a region some 250 miles north and south by 300 miles east and west, where summer heats are sufficient to continuously ripen grain, and to render cultivation profitable. The lands in this tract are within the belt of fairly sufficient and well distributed rainfall—that is, possessed of a fertile soil, and south of the line occupied by the summer isotherm of 65°. These lands may include from 25 to 30 per cent. of a land surface of 100,000 square miles, or from 16,000,000 to 18,000,000 acres. Available data respecting temperatures, rainfall, and the really cultivable portion of the surface, do not warrant a more liberal estimate.

One point that seems to have wholly escaped the attention of Canadians and others—that makes for profitable wheat culture in this northern region —is the well-established physiological fact that, the nearer any of the great staples are grown to their northern or cold limit of production, the greater is the acre yield on land of given fertility. This is the

chief reason why the average yield of wheat per
acre in Ontario and Manitoba is about one-half
greater than in the United States, and not because
of better cultivation in Canada.   The law is equally
definite in the case of cotton; in Arkansas, with a
large population of emancipated slaves, and in the
Indian territory with Indian cultivators, are found
the poorest farming in all the United States, yet in
these two districts the yield of cotton per acre is
greater than elsewhere, except from the deltaic
lands of Egypt.   Not because of better soil or
better culture, but because the lands are near the
northern limit of production.   This law accounts
for greater acre-yields of wheat in Germany than in
France, and for greater acre-yields in Denmark than
in the British Isles, as it also does for better yields
of maize in Nebraska and Iowa than in Kansas and
Missouri.

I have received from Mr R. F. Stupart, Director
of the Meteorological Service, Dominion of Canada,
reports and maps of isothermal lines, showing the
normal temperature of the Dominion for the months
of June, July, August; and Mr C. Wood Davis
has supplemented these with a table giving the
mean temperatures for July and August for terms
of years ranging from two to twenty-five.   These
observations show that from one-half to one-third

only of Manitoba is adapted to wheat—the south-
west portion, now so completely occupied. Probably
from one-sixth to one-third of Assiniboia, the south-
east corner will prove to be a good wheat region.
Although temperatures in most years are sufficiently
high to mature the grain in the south half of that
territory, the rainfall is deficient 150 miles west of
the eastern boundary, and in the northern part of
the district the temperature renders wheat growing
extra hazardous. Limited sheltered districts, or
those of low altitude, may answer for wheat in
Saskatchewan; but these plots, with available
portions of Manitoba and Assiniboia, practically
constitute the whole of the potentially wheat-
bearing Canadian North-West—unless by a miracle
wheat will flourish there at lower temperatures than
elsewhere. Excluding from the table the last three
Manitobian stations—those on the extreme north of
the cultivated district—we have a mean for Manitoba
of nearly 65° F. for the two ripening months. Yet,
under these conditions, in some years the lack of
required heat reduces the crop one-half. Clearly
Manitoba has not a single degree too much; this
being the case in the southern occupied districts,
little wheat can be grown in that province north of
latitude 51°.

TABLE XVI.

Mean Temperatures for July and August for Terms of Years ranging from Two to Twenty-five.

MANITOBA.

Stations	Altitude	Latitude	Longitude	Mean temp. for July	Mean temp. for August	Mean temp. for July and August	No. of years observed
	Feet						
Emerson	...	49°01'	97°13'	67.1	63.8	65.6	3
Treherne	...	49 38	98 42	65.5	60.6	63.1	2
St Albans	...	49 43	99 33	67.7	64.0	65.9	2
Brandon	1176	49 51	99 57	64.3	62.8	63.6	9
Winnipeg	760	49 53	97 07	66.2	63.5	64.9	25
Fort Osborne	...	49 53	97 11	66.6	64.2	65.3	13
Portage la Prairie	830	49 57	98 10	65.8	64.2	65.0	10
Elkhorn	...	49 58	101 16	64.5	61.9	63.2	7
Stony Mountain	803	50 50	97 12	67.5	62.9	65.2	17
Minnedosa	1690	50 10	99 48	62.2	59.5	60.9	15
Russell	1820	50 59	101 20	61.9	57.7	59.9	10
Channel Island	710	52 18	97 23	64.8	63.3	64.1	10
MEANS				65.3	62.4	63.9	10

ASSINIBOIA.

Stations	Altitude	Latitude	Longitude	Mean temp. for July	Mean temp. for August	Mean temp. for July and August	No. of years observed
Alameda	...	49°15'	102°09'	64.1	59.7	61.9	4
Cannington Manor	...	50 00	102 30	63.8	60.2	62.0	3
Medicine Hat	2161	50 01	110 37	67.6	66.0	66.7	14
Swift Current	2439	50 20	107 45	66.2	64.1	65.1	12
Chaplin	2202	50 27	106 49	63.7	63.7	63.7	11
Regina	1885	50 27	104 37	65.2	62.4	63.8	11
Indian Head	1924	50 28	103 40	66.3	62.3	64.3	8
Moose Jaw	1745	50 21	105 35	—	—	—	—
Qu' Appelle	2115	50 44	103 42	63.5	61.5	62.5	15
Henrietta	...	51 22	108 30	64.6	59.9	62.3	5
MEANS				65.0	62.2	63.6	9

TABLE XVI.—*continued.*

SASKATCHEWAN.

Stations	Altitude	Latitude	Longitude	Mean temp. for July	Mean temp. for August	Mean temp. for July and August	No. of years observed
	Feet						
Duck Lake . .	...	52°28'	105°50'	62.8	59.6	61.2	2
Battleford . .	1620	52 41	108 30	64.4	62.6	63.5	5
Prince Albert . .	1402	52 55	106 00	61.9	58.8	60.4	13
Oonikup . .	...	53 30	101 20	62.8	58.4	60.4	6
Cumberland House	900	53 57	102 20	61.8	59.5	60.7	2
Norway House .	400	54 00	98 00	63.5	61.2	62.4	7
MEANS				62.9	60.0	61.5	6

ALBERTA.

Stations	Altitude	Latitude	Longitude	Mean temp. for July	Mean temp. for August	Mean temp. for July and August	No. of years observed
Yarrow . . .	...	49°40'.	115°42'.	61.2	58.8	60.0	2
Macleod . .	...	49 49	113 24	69.5	67.6	68.6	2
Calgary . . .	3389	51 04	114 04	60·4	59.4	59.9	3
Banff . . .	...	51 10	115 35	56.6	56.3	56.5	3
Kneehill . .	...	51 55	113 50	62.2	62.2	62.2	2
Edmonton . .	2158	53 13	113 30	60.6	59.0	59.8	15
MEANS				61.8	60.6	61.2	5

ATHABASCA AND MACKENZIE RIVER.

Stations	Altitude	Latitude	Longitude	Mean temp. for July	Mean temp. for August	Mean temp. for July and August	No. of years observed
Fort Chipewyan .	700	58°43'	111°48'	63.0	58.1	60.5	1
,, ,, .	...	58 42	111 10	58.1	58.0	58.1	3
Peace River . .	Unknown.			57.1	61.7	59.4	1
Fort Franklin .	500	65 12	123 13	52.1	50.6	51.4	· 2
Fort Simpson .	400	61 51	121 57	61.0	53.8	57.4	3
MEANS				58.3	56.4	57.4	2

In tabulating the temperatures, some Hudson's Bay Co.'s figures have been added for Forts Chipewyan, Franklin, and Simpson—the available records in relation to the Peace River and Mackenzie River districts. Limited as are data of this kind, they indicate conditions that would preclude wheat culture on a commercial scale, except in sheltered valleys with a southern exposure.

In several districts the lower latitudes have been placed at the top of the table, to show how temperatures decline as we move north, although this declination is modified in a most striking manner by altitude, as in the case of Channel Island in Manitoba—its altitude being lowest while its latitude is highest. It is in the middle of the southern end of Lake Winnipeg, and the vicinity of water further modifies the climate in summer. Altitude seems as effective as latitude in determining temperatures and wheat-growing capabilities, although Macleod has probably a high altitude while showing a high mean. This is due to its enclosure in a mountain cove.

There may be doubters who will dismiss Reclus as an authority, but few Canadians will question the official " Handbook " of the Dominion. In its description of the North-West Provinces, the " Handbook " says, in substance of Assiniboia, "that the eastern and western portions show marked differences both in climate and topographical features ; that the portion for some 120 miles west of the eastern boundary is practically a continuation to the westward of the grain-growing

areas of Manitoba, and although the soil is somewhat lighter than the deep black loam of the Red
River Valley, it is very warm and productive. . . .
That the western two-thirds of Assiniboia is almost
entirely composed of open plains broken here and
there by ranges of hills. . . . That Southern
Alberta is essentially a ranching (cattle growing)
country, offering unequal opportunities in that
direction, the rainfall being but 12 inches per
annum, and too light to ensure good crops at all
times, but that this aridity constitutes its chief
value as a grazing region. That Northern Alberta
is well adapted to grain-growing "—by which is
probably meant other grains than wheat, as the
summer isotherm of 65° lies but little north of
Edmonton. Barley and oats ripen at a much lower
temperature than wheat.

Of the Province or district of Saskatchewan,
the "Handbook" affirms that "a considerable
portion is a wooded region unadapted to immediate settlement, while the southern portion
closely resembles Northern Alberta, although in
parts the soil is lighter, and in the neighbourhood
of Battleford, as well as in the south-west corner
of the district, the rainfall is at times insufficient
to mature crops." The district of Athabasca is
dismissed with the statement that it is beyond

the trend of probable settlement in the near future.

Richardson, in his " Arctic Expedition," says that tropical temperatures obtain in the Saskatchewan region for a day or two, or for a few hours at a time, yet the three summer months seldom pass without night frosts which destroy tender plants, and in untoward seasons injure the growth of the cerealia ; but it is noted that wheat ripens well in the drier of the limestone districts, and better still in the prairie country. To this it may be added that the summer isotherm of 65° is found at something less than a hundred miles north of Battleford, or Carlton House, its trend being north from about the middle of Lake Winnipeg to a point in lat. 58° 30′ and long. 114°, or a little north of Edmonton, from whence it turns sharply south. Thus nearly all British Columbia, except the small coastal region south of the Fraser River is not only north of that isotherm, but north of the summer isotherm of 60°, and well outside the wheat belt even were surfaces susceptible of cultivation.

Within the limits of Assiniboia, Alberta, and Saskatchewan there are 303,000 square miles of surface, of which some 200,000 seem to be outside the districts of profitable wheat growing.   If, of the remainder, 18,000,000 acres can be brought under all grain crops, it will be as much as can be expected in thirty years.

"Beerbohm" AND FRENCH OFFICIAL RETURNS.

Beerbohm's Evening Corn Trade List for 28th October 1898 says :—

"Nobody will disagree with his (Sir William Crookes's) dictum that the use of artificial manure will come to the rescue. We see this already in France, where an average yield of 22 to 25 bushels per acre is now obtained by higher farming, compared with 15 to 18 bushels only ten years ago. We do not agree with Sir William, however, when he says the consumption of wheat *per capita* in England has been increasing of late years, and that it is now 6 bushels. We believe, on the contrary, that mainly owing to the abundance and cheapness of meat, and the better condition of the working classes, the consumption of bread has actually decreased of late years ; and we believe, too, that before the era of wheat famine, which he foresees, arrives, maize and its products will enter largely into consumption, and so eke out the supplies of wheat in future years."

While *Beerbohm* concedes the possibility and probability of artificial fertilisation postponing the danger of wheat dearth, yet this authority is not in accord with official French reports. Referring to French data it appears that during the ten years ending 1890, some 2,998,000,000 imperial bushels of wheat were grown upon 172,200,000 French acres; the yield from the ten harvests averaging 17.4 imperial bushels per acre—the smallest yield, from the harvest of 1881, being 15.5. Official French returns also show that during the seven years ending 1897, some 116,800,000 French acres were planted with wheat, and produced 2,026,000,000 imperial bushels; the yield averaging 17.3 bushels an acre for the seven harvests, or one-tenth of a bushel less than in the preceding ten years, while the crop of 1897 gave acre yields about a fourth of a bushel less than in 1881!

ACRE YIELDS OF WHEAT.

In a subsequent issue *Beerbohm* expresses surprise that the production of wheat per acre in Belgium has in recent years exceeded that of New Zealand, stating they have always believed in this respect that New Zealand yields were only second to those of the United Kingdom! As Denmark has for 30 years at least given larger acre yields of wheat than those of Great Britain, there must be something radically wrong with the statistics whence *Beerbohm* draws its inspiration.

Unit Consumption of Wheat in the United Kingdom.

It would have been an easy matter for *Beerbohm* absolutely to determine whether unit consumption of wheat in the United Kingdom has or has not increased in recent years; also whether it is or is not now 6 bushels per annum. Such determination requires only the tabulation of official data readily available, as I show in the following tables covering two recent periods, wherein the flour imported is included in equivalent weights of grain, and the net imports are the residue of the gross after deducting foreign, colonial, British and Irish wheat and flour exported year by year.

TABLE XVII.

UNITED KINGDOM.

Wheat Grown, Imported, and Available for Consumption.

(Wheat Grown stated in Imperial Bushels, and Imports in Bushels of 60 lbs.)

Year	Population [1]	Acres employed	Wheat grown	Net imports	Available for consumption
			Bushels	Bushels	Bushels
1884	35,724,000	2,746,000	82,067,000	121,975,000	204,042,000
1885	36,016,000	2,549,000	79,636,000	151,627,000	231,263,000
1886	36,314,000	2,355,000	63,348,000	122,267,000	185,615,000
1887	36,599,000	2,385,000	76,225,000	147,590,000	223,815,000
1888	36,881,000	2,663,000	74,493,000	148,268,000	222,761,000
1889	37,179,000	2,539,000	75,884,000	145,456,000	221,340,000
1890	37,485,000	2,479,000	75,994,000	151,890,000	227,884,000
TOTALS	256,198,000	17,716,000	527,647,000	989,073,000	1,516,720,000
Seed required at 2.5 bushels an acre					44,290,000
Available for consumption other than as seed . . .					1,472,430,000

Average annual unit supply, *exclusive* of seed, 5.747 bushels, or 344.8 lbs.
Average annual unit supply, *including* seed, 5.920 bushels, or 355 lbs.
Average annual *seed* requirements per unit, 0.173 of a bushel, and being 2.9 per cent. of the units' entire quota.

[1] Population figures are taken from the Reports of the Registrar-General, and do not include the population of the islands in the British seas, nor the portions of the Army, Navy, and Merchant Marine abroad.

TABLE XVIII.

UNITED KINGDOM.

Year	Population [1]	Acres employed	Wheat grown	Net imports	Available for consumption
			Bushels	Bushels	Bushels
1891	37,797,000	2,388,000	74,743,000	164,867,000	239,610,000
1892	38,107,000	2,295,000	60,775,000	175,661,000	236,436,000
1893	38,432,000	1,953,000	50,913,000	172,584,000	223,497,000
1894	38,776,000	1,977,000	60,704,000	178,597,000	239,301,000
1895	39,136,000	1,454,000	38,285,000	198,264,000	236,549,000
1896	39,452,000	1,732,000	58,247,000	183,561,000	241,808,000
TOTALS	231,700,000	11,799,000	343,667,000	1,073,534,000	1,417,201,000

Seed required at 2.5 bushels an acre   29,497,000

Available for consumption other than as seed . . .   1,387,704,000

Average annual unit supply, *exclusive* of seed, 5.989 bushels, or 359.3 lbs.
Average annual unit supply, *including* seed, 6.117 bushels, or 367 lbs.
Average annual *seed* requirements, per unit, 0.128 of a bushel, and being 2.1 per cent. of the unit's entire quota.

These tables not only prove that the supply available for food has increased, but that such increase has risen to 14.6 lbs. per annum per unit, or 4.2 per cent. It was stated in my Address that—

"Since 1871 unit consumption of wheat, *including seed*, has slowly increased in the United Kingdom to the present amount of 6 bushels per head per annum."

The supply, including seed, having been equal

[1] Population figures are taken from the Reports of the Registrar-General, and do not include the population of the islands in the British seas, nor the portions of the Army, Navy, and Merchant Marine abroad.

to 6.117 bushels per unit per annum for the six years ending 1896, it follows that my statement was correct, at least as far as relates to the thirteen years ending 1896.

As the British unit's food supply has increased some 14.6 lbs. within thirteen years, it becomes absolutely necessary annually to provide greater quantities of wheat.

Owing to the relative decrease of seed requirements, both by reason of an increase of population and a decrease of acres employed, the unit's entire ration (for both seed and bread) increased but 12 lbs., or in the equivalent of 8,000,000 bushels for a population of 40,000,000. That is to say, an addition of 12 lbs. to unit requirements for seed and food necessitates our seeking yearly abroad an additional 8,000,000 bushels of wheat.

A similar increase of the unit's wheat ration occurs in most of the bread-eating countries, and the increase is bound to continue so long as the relative supply of rye and other bread-making grains decreases. There has been an enormous increase, estimated at 180,000,000 bushels, since 1871, in the "bread-eating world's" annual requirements for wheat independent of the increase resulting from an increase of population. In Britain, the increase is partly due to the marked improvement in the condition of the working classes. Instead of an increase of meat consumption indicating a decrease of wheat consumption, the demand for both commodities has been concurrent in various countries — notably in Denmark. Both demands result from the same cause—increased purchasing power, and the substitution of high for low forms of food.

Eking out supplies of wheat with maize and its products would imply scarcity of wheat, and scarcity of wheat is all that I foresaw, except the possible necessity, consequent on scarcity, of resorting to less sustaining foods.

The World's Wheat Crop of 1897-98.

The *Statist*, 24th September 1898, writes as follows :—

" Sir William may or may not be correct when he says that the numbers of bread-eaters in the world is 516,500,000, but to attempt to estimate the *per capita* consumption is difficult, because it varies considerably. For instance, during the past season it has probably been 10 per cent. below the average of the previous six years ; and 10 per cent. on the crop of the world is no less than 30,000,000 quarters. Sir William is, however, quite wrong in saying that the (world) crop of 1897-98 was only 1,921,000,000 bushels, or 240,000,000 quarters ; the total was not less than 280,000,000 quarters."

It is no more difficult to estimate average annual unit consumption for considerable terms of years than for the *Statist* to say that the entire world's yield of wheat in 1897-98 exceeded 1,921,000,000 bushels by 40,000,000 quarters.

Ascertaining from census tables the population of the important regions inhabited by the bread-eaters of Caucasian race, and extracting from official data the wheat production in such regions, as well as the extent of imports from Southern Asia and North Africa, we have sound foundations for an estimate of average annual unit consumption.

Possibly, as the *Statist* points out, unit consumption of wheat was 10 per cent. less in the 1897-98 harvest than the annual average of the preceding six years. If, however, such decline occurred, especially in the United Kingdom, it ought not to be difficult to show, approximately, so remarkable a reduction as one-tenth in the unit's bread-ration ; the proof needs but the labour involved in the tabulation from official data of the product of wheat in the United Kingdom, and the net imports for the six years, and the last separately. Such a tabulation for the six years as is embodied

in another part of this paper would show that
during the six years ending with 1896 the supply
available for consumption in the United Kingdom
averaged 236,200,000 bushels per annum, while
the supply of 1897, derived from the same sources,
aggregated 219,800,000 bushels—a difference of
16,400,000, just 6.9 per cent. below the average
of the preceding six years. If we take the harvest
year ending August 1898, as a basis of comparison
with the six calendar years ending 1896, we shall
find that the supply from the home harvest and
net imports aggregated 229,200,000 bushels, or
7,000,000 bushels less than the average supply of
the preceding six years. Ascertaining the relative
unit supply, it is found that in the six years, for
bread and seed, it equalled 367 lbs. per annum,
while for the 1897-98 harvest year it dwindled
to 343.8 lbs., or 6.3 per cent. less. In other words,
the result varies but 0.6 per cent. from that based
on the calendar year 1897. Therefore it is mani-
fest that the unit supply could not have been more
than 7 per cent. below that of the six preceding
years even in appearance ; in reality, it was hardly
1 per cent. below. Authorities—without exception—
agree that both the visible and invisible reserve
was reduced enormously in the 1897-98 harvest
year—probably nearly or quite in the full measure

of 23.2 lbs. for each unit of a population of 40,000,000, or by 15,500,000 bushels. Similar conditions doubtless existed elsewhere, but not as readily observable, because a smaller proportion of the supply is derived from external sources, and data are not as available.

DECREASE OF WHEAT CULTIVATION IN THE BRITISH ISLES.

The *Newcastle Journal*, 9th September 1898, writes :—

" Sir William Crookes goes confidently over the whole field, so as to bring out his conclusion that we are within a very short distance of a bread famine. It hardly looks like this when the production of wheat in the British Isles *has decreased more than fifty per cent.* in a quarter of a century, and that not because the land is exhausted, but because there was so much wheat grown in the world that it would not pay to produce it in England."

The question discussed in the Address was not whether it was or was not profitable to grow wheat on British acres, or whether it was most profitable for Britons to import wheat or other products as essential as wheat, but whether there is or is not sufficient available wheat-growing land in the world fit to provide a regular annual unit supply, for a population increasing by progressively greater annual aggregates, equalling the 4.5 bushels available in 1898 for each unit of the 516,500,000 constituting the bread-eating populations of Caucasian race. This problem involves the continued power to command unit supplies of other food staples equalling those now available by such populations, as well as of equivalent supplies of the fibres produced in the temperate zones.

As the *Newcastle Journal* attributes the reduction of British wheat-fields, as well as the non-expansion of others, to deficient prices, it is well to ascertain what other British crop areas have diminished and what expanded, together with the ratios of increase and decrease relative to population, and whether we should not be required to import the products of an equal number of acres regardless whether such imports were wheat or other indispensable soil products. Much light can be thrown on this interesting and hitherto little considered point by the official comparison of the crop distribution of 1871 and 1897. The following table deals exclusively with Great Britain, as not until long after 1871 were data relative to the Irish hay area available :—

TABLE XIX.

Crop Distribution in Great Britain in 1871 *and* 1897.

Description of crop	1871	1897	Increases and decreases	Percentage of change
	Acres	Acres		
Wheat . . .	3,572,000	1,889,000	1,683,000 −	47.1 −
Barley . . .	2,385,000	2,036,000	349,000 −	14.6 −
Oats	2,716,000	3,036,000	320,000 +	11.8 +
Rye	71,000	76,000	5,000 +	7.1 +
Beans and peas . .	930,000	420,000	510,000 −	54.8 −
TOTALS of corn areas	9,674,000	7,457,000	—	—
Net decrease of acres under corn . .	—	—	2,217,000 −	22.9 −
Potatoes . . .	628,000	505,000	123,000 −	19.5 −
Turnips and mangolds	2,524,000	2,188,000	336,000 −	13.3 −
Cabbage, vetches, etc.	566,000	497,000	69,000 −	12.2 −
Clover, etc., for hay .	2,165,000	2,286,000 ⎫		
Permanent grass, for hay . . .	3,490,000	4,510,000 ⎬	1,141,000 +	20.2 +
Rotation grass, not for hay . .	2,205,000	2,568,000 ⎭		
Permanent grass, not for hay . .	8,946,000	12,003,000	3,420,000 +	30.7 +
Orchards and Market Gardens . .	243,000	321,000	78,000 +	32.1 +
TOTALS other than corn	20,767,000	24,878,000	—	—
Net increase of acres other than corn .	—	—	4,111,000 +	19.8 +
TOTALS of all crop areas	30,441,000	32,335,000	—	—
Net increase of acres under crops [1] .	—	—	1,894,000 +	6.2 +

Increase of Horses and Cattle.

Horses on British farms	1,254,000	1,526,000	272,000 +	21.7 +
Cattle on British farms	5,338,000	6,500,000	1,162,000 +	21.8 +
Cattle imported .	249,000	618,000	369,000 +	148.2 +
Horses imported (in 1883) . . .	10,000	50,000	40,000 +	400.2 +

[1] Pasture treated as a crop, as it is of grass.

TABLE XIX.—*continued.*

Comparative Imports of Grain per Annum in Two Five-Year Periods.

Description of crop	1871-75	1892-96	Increases and decreases	Percentage of change
	Cwts.	Cwts.		
Wheat . . .	50,400,000	98,600,000	48,200,000 +	95.2 +
Barley . . .	11,000,000	22,900,000	11,900,000 +	108.2 +
Oats . . .	11,600,000	15,500,000	3,900,000 +	33.6 +
Maize . . .	19,700,000	37,900,000	18,200,000 +	92.4 +
TOTALS . .	92,700,000	174,900,000	82,200,000 +	88.7 +

These tabulations develop remarkable conditions. While the total of the grain areas has shrunk 22.9 per cent., under other products, including pasture, the areas have increased 19.8 per cent.; the grand total is 6.2 per cent. greater. This increase is all due to the extension of permanent pasture, seemingly in the measure of 1,894,000 acres, independent of a decrease of the corn crops.

Possibly a decrease of about 20 per cent. in the area under potatoes may account for that increase of unit consumption of wheat which the *Statist* and *Beerbohm*, and others, doubt; but potato fields shrinking a fifth while population increases 37 per cent. indicates a substitution for the tuber in the nation's dietary; as it appears the wheat ration has increased, are we not justified in believing that wheat has taken the place of the discarded potatoes?

Other criticisms of portions of my Address by various minor journals can be answered by replying in detail to a few of the points raised in an able and comprehensive article which appeared in *The Times* of 9th September 1898. From this article I quote the following sentences :—

"Why, for instance, should it be assumed that for many years the wheat area of Roumania is not likely to exceed home requirements, when it is admitted that the country has a considerable amount of surplus land which can be used for wheat?"

"Why does Sir William Crookes summarily brush aside the calculation of Professor Shelton, that there are still 50,000,000 acres in Queensland suitable for wheat?"

"What does he make of the statement just telegraphed from Sydney that the wheat-growing area in New South Wales has been increased in a single year by no less than 26 per cent.?"

"Why does he assume that after the customary supply of food has begun to fail, population will still continue to increase at the present rate?"

"Why does he ignore the significance in relation to supply and demand of the fact recorded by himself that the rate of consumption of wheat has risen from 4.15

bushels per unit per annum in 1878 to 4.5 bushels at the present time, and that the area planted with the two great bread-making grains, wheat and rye, is actually less now than eighteen years ago, despite enormous additions to the population?"

Roumania in the Near Future.

My conclusion is warranted by the cessation, eight years ago, of additions to the wheat area; by the fact that Roumanian requirements for wheat increase, not only because of rapid increase of population, but by increase of unit consumption; because the areas under maize, barley, and oats since 1890 have increased respectively 9, 18, and 58 per cent. as a result of a sharp demand for feeding grains at home and in Western Europe; because the areas under such industrial crops as beet, colza, flax, hemp, and tobacco, increase more rapidly than population, and because the hay required by great additions to the flocks and herds absorbs the reduced acres. The hay area alone has increased more than 300,000 acres since 1890, or 28 per cent., and the population being more prosperous than ever before, the standard of living is elevated. A growing demand for a multiplicity of products reflects the prosperity of the Roumanian people and their increasing requirements.

PROFESSOR SHELTON AND THE 50,000,000
QUEENSLAND ACRES.

Mr T. A. Coghlan, Government Statist of New
South Wales, referring to a decrease in the continent's wheat area relatively to population, has
said that :—

" This comparative decrease is owing to various causes.
. . . It is probable that the agricultural returns (of New
South Wales) will show more than usual increase during
the next few years, principally in consequence of the
falling in of pastoral leases in the Eastern Division,
through which large tracts of arable land in close proximity
to extensively settled districts became available for settlement. . . . Taking all the circumstances of the case into
consideration, it is evident that any large extension of
wheat growing (in Australia) cannot be expected, unless
perhaps, in New South Wales, *the only colony which
though adapted to wheat growing, produces less than the
requirements of its population*."

Clearly, Mr Coghlan does not endorse Professor
Shelton's views respecting the possibility of successful wheat culture on a great scale in Queensland.
Wheat has been grown in Queensland for thirty years
or more, but the area sown in any one year has never
exceeded so small a fraction of 50,000,000 acres as
150,000 acres, and only in 1892 and 1896 has so

much of the sown area as 30,000 acres been deemed worth harvesting ; the blighted remainder and that sown for fodder being mown for hay.   The fact is the hot and ·humid climate of Queensland suits the sugar-cane and tropical staples, but plays havoc with wheat.

New South Wales.

This reported increase of 26 per cent. in an area of 866,000 acres is of little moment.   An increase of the Australian wheat area, as a whole, has not only been expected, but its principal location officially and clearly indicated by Mr Coghlan, and in all probability has been produced in part by reducing areas under other products.   It cannot therefore be classed as an addition to the world's food-bearing acres.

Scarcity of Food and Increase of Population.

It is just as likely as not that the present increase in population may continue for the whole or the major part of the next thirty years, even if food becomes somewhat less abundant.   No distressing dearth of foods other than wheat has been suggested within that period.   The teeming

millions of India are always on the verge of dearth,
if not of starvation; yet India's population between
1871 and 1881 increased 11.4 per cent., or at a
rate as great as that now recorded in Europe
as a whole. In Europe the great Russian population increases in a similar ratio, although the mass
of the Russian people are doomed to short rations,
and, as is well known, local famines are not in-
frequent. Even in one of the British Isles, although the population diminishes by emigration, yet
the meagre diet of the peasantry does not prevent
early marriages and the birth of more units than can
be fully fed by an agriculture that seems not too
wisely directed. However, if we base our calculations upon the conservative assumption that the
annual increase of population will be no greater
than at present, the food supply promises to become
a very perplexing problem after another generation have passed away.

SUPPLY AND DEMAND.

I have not ignored the fact that unit consumption of wheat increased from 4.15 bushels in 1878
to 4.5 bushels at the present time, when in the
interim little or no addition was made to the area
under the two greater bread-yielding grains. May

I be permitted to say that in my Address I stated that this anomalous result proceeded from the accident, over world-wide areas, of such favourable climatic conditions from 1882-96 as to give eleven crops of wheat and ten of rye above the average in acre yield—crops, moreover which furnished abundant supplies from their bountiful excess, and served also to mask a great acreage deficit. So anomalous were the conditions that when one crop, that of 1897, showed itself less than 9 per cent. below the twenty-six years' average acre yield, prices rose greatly, reserves everywhere disappeared, and large drafts were made upon the harvest of 1898-99 at least a month earlier than usual. The complete dissipation of reserves by one world harvest less than 9 per cent. below the average in acre yield, when the ten preceding world crops averaged more than 5 per cent. above a twenty-six years' average, shows how near to dearth is the bread-eating world. The enquiry naturally follows as to what might happen should the world successively harvest two such crops as those of 1875 and 1876, which gave acre yields respectively 11.7 and 12 per cent. below the average of the crops harvested from 1871 to 1896? Prices did not then immediately advance, because of plentiful reserves from previous harvests, and because the world's bread-bearing area was not then deficient—as it now so clearly is if we obtain only average acre yields for any considerable term of years.

Of the British areas contributing, either in primary or secondary form to the food supply, we find, in Table XIX., excluding orchards, gardens, and cabbage plots, that none except areas devoted largely to the subsistence of domestic animals, show any sign of increase. The area under oats shows an increase of about 12 per cent., despite an increase in imports of some 34 per cent. This increase, like the increase of imports of barley and maize, is directly due to a rise of 21.7 per cent. in the number of horses and cattle kept upon the farms, and to a rise of even greater proportions in the number of horses in the urban districts. This is indicated by an increase since 1883 of 400 per cent. in the number of imported horses, despite an increase of probably more than 30 per cent. in the number of horses bred for sale. With decreasing tillage the proportion of farm horses reared for sale has doubtless increased disproportionately to the whole number on the farms.

With an increase of 37 per cent. in the population of the United Kingdom, and an increase in the proportion of the well-to-do, the number of town-kept horses has probably risen more than 37 per cent. Hence, even a greater increase in the total supply of the feeding grains—by production and importation—than of wheat, and the necessity of devoting a continuously greater proportion of the land to the subsistence of horses, as, even when imported (unlike animals intended for slaughter) they must be fed.

While British imports of wheat have increased 95 per cent., imports of feeding grains have increased over 80 per cent.; and this, with the increase of oats production, seems to furnish a greater relative supply of other grains than wheat.

Possibly the wheat area has decreased more rapidly than other grain areas, because wheat is more readily stored, and the imported wheat is of relatively better quality than that of oats imported from Russia and much of the barley brought from abroad.

So long as Britain is forced to import cereals in quantities that increase more rapidly than population, it seems to be a matter of no great importance whether imports consist of greater or less proportions of wheat or other staples equally indispensable to civilised life; and it is possible that the only injury the nation will sustain by continuing to grow the needful grass, horses and cattle, and dairy products, will be the loss of employment on the land.

The grass lands of the United Kingdom (the best in the world), excluding those of mountain and heath, are in the proportion of 85 acres to each 100 population units, despite enormous imports of animal products from foreign and colonial meadows and pastures, and in Great Britain itself the ratio of acres under grass is as 260 (rich as they are) to each 100 head of farm horses or cattle.

In 1895 some 628,000,000 acres contributed the grains, cotton, and potatoes consumed by the 497,000,000 units constituting the bread-eating populations of Caucasian race, the proportions being as follows :—

TABLE XX.

	Acres.
Wheat	161,000,000*
Rye	108,000,000
Oats	112,000,000
Maize	113,000,000
Buckwheat, Spelt, and Maslin . .	14,000,000
Barley	50,000,000†
Potatoes	32,000,000
Cotton	32,000,000
TOTAL . . .	628,000,000

* Three million acres represented by imports from Asia and North Africa.

† About 2,000,000 acres of barley also being represented by imports from Asia and North Africa.

The whole area was equivalent to 1.28 acres for the supply of the bread-eating units, and adding grass lands in the ratio of the rich English acres, or 2.6 acres for each of the 240,000,000 farm horses and cattle then owned by bread-eating populations, or 125 acres of meadow and pasture for each 100 units of such populations, no less than 1,260,000,000 actually productive acres then contributed to the subsistence and pleasure of 497,000,000 bread-eaters. This consumption implies annual additions of not less than 16,500,000 equally productive acres (or a greater number of less productive ones) to meet the requirements of annual additions to the bread-eating population no greater than the addition of 6,500,000 units in 1898-99—unless we can devise means of inducing the laborious peasants who grow so great a proportion of the world's products to promptly increase acre yields by improving both culture and fertilisation.

Between 1895—to which year Table XX. relates —and 1898, the wheat area of the world increased by some 4,000,000 acres, while that under rye decreased about 2,500,000 acres. In the United States the area under maize and oats decreased respectively 4,400,000 and 2,200,000 acres.

OUR PRESENT AND PROSPECTIVE FOOD SUPPLY.*

By C. WOOD DAVIS, Kansas, U.S.A.

THE populations of European lineage inhabit-
ing Asiatic Russia, the United States, Canada,
Australasia, Argentina, Chili, Uruguay, Brazil,
South Africa, and Europe and its colonies constitute the world's "bread eaters," as with other
populations grain rarely assumes the form of the
loaf. These "bread eaters" have increased from
371,000,000 in 1870-71 to 520,000,000 in 1899.
The increase is so much more rapid now than in any
preceding age that additions of but little more than
4,000,000 units in 1870-71 have risen now to annual
additions of more than 6,000,000. This progressive
increase necessitates annual additions to the world's
bread supply of 50 per cent. more than sufficed
thirty years ago! Yet, despite this enormous

* Mr C. Wood Davis has been good enough to supplement my
previous statements by the following comprehensive review of the
sources and extent of the world's present and prospective food supply.

134

increase in requirements, little addition has been made to the bread-bearing lands since 1884, as the world area employed in growing bread-making grains proper is barely 2,400,000 acres greater than fifteen years ago, showing an increase of less than one per cent. in area against an increase of 20 per cent. on the part of the consumers.

During the thirteen years ending with 1884 the United States contributed about 20,800,000 new acres to the world's wheat and rye fields, as against a contribution of some 8,800,000 acres by all other regions. In 1884 the States practically ceased to add to the wheat fields, although recently, by diminishing the areas devoted to other staples, they have cultivated a wheat area of 44,100,000 acres in 1898 as against 39,500,000 acres fourteen years earlier. Of this apparent increase, however, about 700,000 acres were diverted from the production of rye, and 200,000 acres from the growth of buck-wheat. As a matter of fact, our *net* additions to the world's bread-bearing area since 1844 aggregate barely 3,700,000 acres, and even this meagre increase has been effected only by reducing by more than 10,000,000 acres the areas devoted to maize, oats, and hay.

Outside the regions inhabited by the bread-eating populations, about 40,000,000 acres are employed, mostly in Southern Asia and North Africa, in the production of wheat. As the bread-eaters derive, however, from these countries less than one per cent. of their supply, it is best to deal with such sources only in respect of the imports therefrom. In the last five years these imports have averaged about 20,000,000 bushels of wheat per annum.

The bread-eating population, and the areas employed in the regions designated as those they inhabit, in growing each of the bread-making grains, have been approximately as follows :*—

TABLE XXI.

	1870-71	1883-84	1898-99	Increases and decreases since 1870-71	Per cent. of change since 1870-71
Population	371,000,000	434,000,000	520,000,000	149,000,000+	39.6+
	Acres	Acres	Acres	Acres	
Wheat .	124,000,000	153,000,000	165,000,000	41,000,000+	33.6+
Rye .	110,000,000	110,000,000	105,500,000	4,500,000-	4.0-
Spelt .	2,300,000	2,100,000	1,900,000	400,000-	17.4-
Maslin .	3,400,000	2,200,000	2,000,000	1,400,000-	41.2-
Buckwheat	16,200,000	14,700,000	9,000,000	7,200,000-	44.4-
Totals .	255,900,000	282,000,000	283,400,000	27,500,000+	10.7+

* As the final revision of some of the data upon which numerical statements are made is as yet incomplete, it should be understood that some of such statements in this paper are but approximations, although the changes resulting from revision have rarely been material.

Against a population increase of 39.6 per cent. since 1871, the area under the bread-making grains proper has increased but 10.7 per cent., showing an acreage deficit of more than 70,000,000 acres!

It is true, that the wheat area has increased 33.6 per cent., but the greater part of this increase occurred in the first half of the period, while it has been accompanied by a decrease of 13,500,000 acres under rye, spelt, maslin, and buckwheat, much of this area having been absorbed by the wheat fields which otherwise would show a much smaller increase.

This table shows clearly that the rye, spelt, maslin, and buckwheat lands in 1871 constituted 52 per cent. of the "bread-bearing" area, while in 1898-99 these lands constituted but 41 per cent. of such area. This little-considered change has thrown an enormous additional duty upon wheat, which now constitutes about 60 per cent. of all the bread-making material as against less than 50 per cent. thirty years ago. This pressure is also increased by the fact that the wheat fields long since ceased to expand in a ratio equalling the increase of population, although swollen by great drafts upon the rye, spelt, maslin, and buckwheat fields. This extra duty imposed upon wheat has increased annual requirements for that grain by more than

180,000,000 bushels, aside from any increase of
annual requirements resulting from an increase of
population. · This increase of 180,000,000 bushels
results from a reduction in the unit's quota of the
other bread-making grains, and is directly due to a
reduction of the rye, spelt, maslin, and buckwheat
areas relatively to population.

As rye, spelt, maslin, and buckwheat are grown
for human food as exclusively as wheat, a shrinkage
in the areas under those grains of 10,600,000 acres
since 1884 reduces the net increase of the world's
" bread-bearing " lands in the last fifteen years to
barely 2,400,000 acres, or less than one per cent.,
as against a population increase of 20 per cent. ; and
this despite the increase of the wheat areas of
Canada, Australasia, Argentina, and Siberia, about
which so much has been said.   Indeed, the additions
in these regions since 1884 have been only equivalent
to the requirements of the last two years' increased
population of bread eaters, while in Europe there
has been great shrinkage of areas under other bread-
making grains.   Bearing in mind the fact that the
bread   eaters   require   an   average   annual   unit
supply of the bread-making grains equal to the
net product from 0.67 of an acre, and remembering
that 86,000,000 bread eaters have been added since
1884, we see in the following table how comparatively

insignificant have been the additions made to the wheat-bearing areas of the above-named countries since 1884 :—

TABLE XXII.

	1883-84	1898-99	Increase
	Acres	Acres	Acres
Canada * . .	2,400,000	3,200,000	800,000
Australasia .	3,200,000	4,500,000	1,300,000
Argentina . .	1,400,000	6,100,000	4,700,000
Siberia . .	2,000,000	3,300,000	1,300,000
Totals . .	9,000,000	17,100,000	8,100,000

From the harvesting of the great world crop of 1882—a crop aggregating some 320,000,000 bushels above the average of the three preceding years—the price fell until 1890. The moderate crops of 1889, 1890, and 1891—together but 1.7 per cent. above the average—resulted in moderately higher prices, as the " remainders " from the great world crops of 1882, 1884, 1887, and 1888 were being absorbed. This absorption was complete by harvest time in 1891, a year which is generally held to have been one of famine, although the world's out-turn per acre in 1891 was actually above the twenty-seven years' average of 12.7 bushels an acre. As a matter of

* The wheat acreage of Canada increased about 300,000 acres in 1898, but largely by the substitution of wheat for other staples.

fact, the famine of 1891 was not a wheat but a rye famine, rye throughout the 1891-92 harvest year bearing a higher price than wheat in many of the markets of continental Europe. Despite the general belief that there was a defective wheat world harvest in 1891, it was not only above the average of the last twenty-eight years in acre yield, but was larger than either of the three immediately preceding harvests. Only two of the preceding twenty world harvests exceeded it in volume, while but five out of the twenty exceeded it in acre yield! The world, however, had even then outgrown its wheat-bearing area. An average yield an acre from the areas now employed would give an aggregate quite 250,000,000 bushels below the requirements of 1899-1900! In other words, the wheat area alone is now deficient— for net average yields—by more than 24,000,000 acres, while the rye, spelt, maslin, and buckwheat areas are defective by even a greater area. We see the result in a chronic rye famine in Russia for the past ten years!

The bread-eating world's experience in 1891 shows, quite as conclusively as its more recent experience in 1897, how very close to distressing dearth its rapidly increasing population lives, and indicates the serious results likely to follow the harvesting of two world crops in succession giving acre yields no greater than that of 1897,—but 8.8 per cent. below the average. In the eighth decade of the century four world harvests gave acre yields from 11.7 per cent. to 12.5 per cent. below the 27 years' average ; and a succession of world harvests as defective as those of the eighth decade are just as probable as a succession of " over-average " crops such as we have had in the last nine years, when eight harvests combined were 6.8 per cent. in excess of average from 1,280,000,000 acres, yielding aggregate *over-average* product of no less than 1,100,000,000 bushels.

Deducting a deficit of 190,000,000 in the harvest of 1897, the net " over-average " wheat production of the last nine years has been 910,000,000 bushels. We can form some idea of what would have been the conditions of bread supply, and the price of wheat, had the harvests from 1890 to 1898 inclusive given acre yields no greater than the average of the last twenty-eight years!

Over-average acre yields have for many years prevented scarcity, but the potent and distress-saving factor since 1870 has been the immense increase of the grain-growing area of the United States. To get a clear conception of the relative increase of the food-bearing areas of the whole bread-eating-world, and of the United States, it is probably best

to show the additions since 1870, and the proportion
contributed by the United States.   The bread-eating
world's grain and potato-bearing areas have been as
shown in the following Table, while those of the
United States are shown in Table XXIV., p. 148.

TABLE XXIII.

The Food-Bearing Area of the Bread-Eating World.

	POPULATION			Increases and decreases since 1870-71	Per cent. of change since 1870-71
	1870-71	1883-84	1898-99		
	371,000,000	434,000,000	520,000,000	149,000,000 +	39.6 +
	Acres	Acres	Acres	Acres	
Wheat	124,000,000	153,000,000	165,000,000	41,000,000 +	33.6 +
Rye	110,000,000	110,000,000	105,500,000	4,500,000 –	4.0 –
Barley	43,700,000	43,300,000	47,100,000	3,400,000 +	7.7 +
Oats	84,400,000	103,000,000	109,000,000	24,600,000 +	29.1 +
Maize	55,700,000	96,200,000	107,500,000	51,800,000 +	93.0 +
Spelt	2,300,000	2,100,000	1,900,000	400,000 –	17.4 –
Maslin	3,400,000	2,200,000	2,000,000	1,400,000 –	41.2 –
Buckwheat	16,200,000	14,700,000	9,000,000	7,200,000 –	44.4 –
Potatoes	23,300,000	27,200,000	32,000,000	8,700,000 +	37.3 +
Totals	463,000,000	551,700,000	579,000,000	116,000,000 +	25.1 +

Additions to bread eaters since 1871 are about
149,000,000, or 39.6 per cent., while additions to
the food-bearing areas are but 116,000,000 acres,
or 25.1 per cent.   It therefore follows that the
relative increase has been about in the ratio of five

to eight! Probably the most significant point in the table is, that maize only, of the nine staples, has increased at a rate equalling that of the population; and this product is devoted almost wholly to the production of such secondary commodities as meat, lard, glucose, starch, and spirits, and the feeding of dairy, draft, and pleasure animals. Another significant fact is that potatoes, the most quickly perishable product, bearing neither prolonged storage nor transport over world-wide distances, have, next to maize, most nearly kept pace with the rate of population increase, while oats, the great feeding grain of which Europe grows about three-fourths as many acres as it does of wheat, have increased at a rate a fourth less than the population rate. A fact nearly as significant in many respects is, that till 1884 the areas devoted to the production of grains and potatoes in the regions inhabited by the bread eaters were equivalent to more than 1.26 acres for each population unit, while the acres added since 1884 would give each added unit but 0.36 of an acre of the same products. Even if we divide the old areas and additions made since 1884 equally between the 520,000,000 units to be fed at the present time, this would give each but 1.12 acres, indicating an area deficit of the great primary food staples of some 74,000,000 acres.

It is obvious from the data in Tables No. XXI. and XXIII. that either the acreage was largely excessive from 1871 to 1884, or that it is now greatly deficient. That it was not excessive prior to 1884 is clearly shown by the fact that there then existed no over-abundant supply of any of the staples included in the tables, as well as by the closely related and indicative fact that prices for such staples, in the entire period between 1871 and 1884, bore prices ranging from 50 to 150 per cent. higher than they have been since 1892. The apparent anomaly of over-abundant supplies, in recent years, from a largely deficient acreage results from the character of acre yields, which have been greatly above the twenty-eight years' average in nearly three-fourths of the years since 1883. These extraordinary yields have been due to exceptionally favourable climatic conditions over world-wide areas in eleven out of the last fifteen years ; so that eleven of the wheat harvests, and ten of the rye, oats, and barley harvests, have given yields so much above the twenty-eight years' average as to completely mask a great and constantly increasing area deficit.

Notwithstanding the exceptional yields from the last fifteen harvests, exports of both the bread-making and feeding grains from America have increased with astonishing rapidity. This is notably true of

the feeding grains, exports of which have increased
more rapidly than those of wheat, because the swine
and horses and the dairy animals in many European
countries have increased faster than the population.
Hence Europe's rapidly increasing demand for
feeding-stuffs will largely absorb the produce of all
the acreage which both North and South America
can possibly spare for export.

Since May 1896 the United States have exported
to Europe 710,000,000 bushels of such feeding
grains as maize, oats, and barley, or more than three
times as much as in any other three successive
years since 1879, whilst in the last three years their
contributions of wheat and rye to the bread
supply of Europe have been 520,000,000 bushels.
Enormous as this quantity seems to be, yet,
contrary to universal belief, America's contributions
to Europe's supply of the bread-making and
feeding grains have recently been in the ratio of
5 to 7!

Respecting the demand for feeding grains, it
should be said that it is just as imperative as that
for bread-stuffs, as the supply of meat, and dairy
and other products (as essential to civilised life as
bread) depends in most regions upon an adequate
supply of these grains. Europe, finding it necessary
to provide more pasturage and hay than heretofore,

is becoming more and more dependent upon outside sources for maize, oats, and barley.

The belief is common, if not universal, that in the
event of wheat becoming relatively less abundant,
scarcity may most easily be prevented by the
substitution of other grains, the only result being
changes, held to be immaterial, in individual and
national dietaries. This position, however, is
wholly untenable, as to provide an equivalent
nutriment in other forms will necessitate the use of
quite as much land. That is, the acreage and cost
will be as great as with the continued use of
wheat, which can be grown quite as readily
as the other grains in most regions. Moreover, if
bread eaters are to have their accustomed supplies
of animal products, and be able to command animal
services as heretofore, the acres under maize, oats,
barley, hay, and pasturage must be at least in the
same ratio to population as now ; hence these acres
must increase at a rate equalling that of the
population. As there is now no surplus of these
products the substitution of other grains for wheat
on any considerable scale is obviously impracticable,
while the necessary change of diet would be wholly
unacceptable unless compensated for by an improb-
ably great reduction in both land and money cost.

Under existing conditions respecting occupancy

and employment of lands of the temperate zones, and the increase of population, it is the inevitable tendency of all grains to become less abundant relatively to requirements.

Thirty years ago enormous drafts were made upon the exceptionally fertile plains and valleys of North America, resulting in additions to the food-bearing and fibre-bearing areas of the temperate zones sufficient to provide food and raiment for a great part of the 149,000,000 units since added to the bread eaters. Similar drafts are now impossible in any part of the world, as in the two temperate zones there do not exist as many unemployed acres equal in productive power to these brought under cultivation in the last thirty years. But the necessity for such additions will become more and more imperative as population continues to increase.

It is possible to give a fairly clear conception of probable additions to the food-bearing area by showing what has been done in that direction since 1870. So far as the bread-eating world as a whole is concerned, this is shown in Table No. XXIII., from which it appears that between 1870-71 and 1883-84 additions to the food-bearing lands averaged 6,800,000 acres per annum, while they were but 2,000,000 acres per annum from 1883-84 to

1898-99 ! It will be interesting, if not instructive, to learn what part and what proportion of the added acres were contributed by the United States, and what by the rest of the bread-eating world. This will show to what insignificant proportions the contributions of the United States have shrunk since 1889.

This last feature is shown clearly in your Table No. XII., a copy of which you kindly sent me (*see* page 59).

The data for the periods between 1870-71 and 1883-84, and between 1883-84 and 1898-99, are given in the following table :—

TABLE XXIV.

The Food-Bearing Areas of the United States.

	1870-71	1883-84	1898-99	Acres added since 1870-71	Per cent. of increase
	Acres	Acres	Acres		
Wheat .	19,900,000	39,500,000	44,100,000	24,200,000	121.6
Rye . .	1,100,000	2,300,000	1,600,000	500,000	45.5
Barley .	1,200,000	2,600,000	2,600,000	1,400,000	116.6
Oats .	8,400,000	21,300,000	25,800,000	17,400,000	207.1
Maize .	34,100,000	69,700,000	77,700,000	43,600,000	127.9
Buckwheat	400,000	900,000	700,000	300,000	75.0
Potatoes .	1,200,000	2,200,000	2,600,000	1,400,000	116.6
Totals .	66,300,000	138,500,000	155,100,000	88,800,000	133.9

Since 1871 88,800,000 acres, or an increase of

133.9 per cent., have been added to the food-bearing area of the United States, but of this total no less than 72,200,000 acres were added in the thirteen years ending 1884, and 14,200,000 acres in the five years ending 1889; while in the last ten years barely 2,400,000 acres have been added, or less than sufficient to meet the requirements of one year's addition to the home population. Even this insignificant addition of the last ten years has been rendered possible only by a reduction of 10,000,000 acres in the area devoted to hay; effected by reducing herds of domestic animals below normal requirements, by slaughtering a vast proportion of the foundation or breeding stock, with a consequent rapid advance in prices. The hay lands diverted to the production of the great primary food staples, and to the minor products required by a rapidly increasing home population, are likely to revert, so far as they can be spared from present use, to their former employment, as strenuous efforts are being made to increase the herds—an increase which cannot proceed far without increasing the dry forage.

Of an increase of 116,000,000 acres since 1871 in the food-bearing areas of the bread-eating world, as shown in Table No. XXIII., the United States has contributed 77 per cent. It has contributed 59 per

cent. of all additions to the wheat fields ; 41 per
cent. of the increase of the area under barley ; 71
per cent. of the additions to the oats lands, and no
less than 84 per cent. of the acres brought under
maize. That is, the contribution of the United
States has been 88,800,000 acres as against
27,200,000 in all the other regions inhabited by
bread-eating populations of European lineage !
As our additions have now shrunk to such proportions as to be insufficient for our increasing
home needs, it is altogether probable that we shall
hereafter be forced to make annually increasing
drafts upon lands now employed in growing food
for exportation, in order to give the increased
local population *quotas* of both the major and
minor food staples equalling those heretofore distributed. This phase of the question is treated
in a thorough manner in a subsequent article by
Mr Hyde.

West of the Mississippi, and lying mostly within
the drainage basin of the Missouri River (for convenience, called " the Missouri Valley "), are the
political divisions of Minnesota, Iowa, Missouri,
Kansas, Nebraska, South Dakota, North Dakota,
and Oklahoma, having an area, exclusive of an arid
western border of about 100 miles in width, of
some 300,000,000 acres, or something less than a

sixth of the area of the United States, not counting Alaska and the recently acquired islands.

This region is three times the extent of all the actually or potentially wheat-bearing lands of South America, and is probably the largest continuous body of equally fertile land in either temperate zone. Being mostly a treeless plain over which population could move with the greatest facility, this region was susceptible, as few others are, of the rapid development which here took place since 1865.

In 1870 the Missouri Valley, as a whole, was very sparsely inhabited, and grew but 47,000,000 bushels of wheat on some 3,500,000 acres. Since 1870, however, development has been so rapid, that in 1898 this district had no less than 22,700,000 acres under wheat, yielding 326,000,000 of the 675,000,000 bushels grown in the United States. It comprises more than half the nation's wheat lands, grows 40 per cent. of the oats, more than half the maize entering commercial channels, has 33 per cent. of all the farm horses, and 28 per cent. of the cattle and swine, although it possesses less than 16 per cent. of either the population or land of the Republic.

Thus a region which thirty years ago was in large part the hunting ground of the untutored savage has become the granary of the nation, and grows more wheat, nearly as much oats, and twenty times as much maize as the 112,000,000 inhabitants of all that part of the Russian empire lying north of the Caucasus and west of the Urals ; and this with an industrial, commercial, and agricultural population probably less than 12,000,000.

The communities of the Missouri Valley raising enormous surpluses of grain and meat, which the world must have and can procure nowhere else, and having large and rapidly growing manufacturing ndustries, will become and remain, at least until the local population shall have quintupled, the most prosperous and wealthy in the world. For with the advance in food values, resulting from the disparity in the rate of increase of "food-bearing" acres and "bread-eaters," prices which in so many recent years have been below the cost of production will soon rise to highly profitable levels. Then it will be possible to increase acre yields in the Missouri Valley by applications of fixed nitrogen and of the stores of phosphatic materials abounding in Tennessee and Kentucky—stores which would now return less than the fertilisation would cost.

Comprising more than half the wheat-bearing acres of the nation, the Missouri Valley furnishes from its surplus all the wheat exported, as with only average yields the rest of the Republic grows less wheat than it consumes. Therefore, it is to this remote mid-continent district that Western Europe is indebted for that enormous volume of bread-making and feeding grains which has kept want from its doors for at least a decade.

The following Table shows what additions have been made to the food-bearing areas in the Missouri Valley within the last thirty years, but it must be remembered that additions to the productive area on any considerable scale have now ceased, and are impracticable outside a limited portion of Oklahoma :—

TABLE XXV.

Food-Bearing Areas of the Missouri Valley.

Product	1870-71	1898-99	Increase of acres since 1870-71	Per cent. of increase
	Acres	Acres		
Wheat . . .	3,500,000	22,700,000	19,200,000	549.1
Maize . . .	6,900,000	32,100,000	25,200,000	365.2
Oats . . .	1,200,000	10,700,000	9,500,000	791.7
Barley . . .	100,000	1,100,000	1,000,000	1000.0
Rye and Buckwheat .	100,000	300,000	200,000	200.0
Potatoes . . .	100,000	600,000	500,000	500.0
Totals . . .	11,900,000	67,500,000	55,600,000	467.2

Of 116,000,000 acres added to the bread-eating world's food-bearing areas since 1871, it has been shown in Table No. XXIV. that the United States contributed 88,800,000, as against 27,200,000 acres by all other parts of the world ; while in the above table it is shown that 55,600,000 out of the 88,800,000 acres must be credited to the eight communities of the Missouri Valley.

Is it not somewhat startling to find that the world's food supply during the last decade of this century has depended so largely upon the rapidity with which it was possible to develop this region ? And is it not even more startling to reflect that in the whole world it will not be possible in the next thirty years to bring under cultivation as many productive acres as have been added in the Missouri Valley since 1871 ? At the same time, the necessity for additions is great on account of the increased annual additions to the bread-eaters ; and still greater owing to an enormous acreage deficit. This deficit will be apparent whenever one world-crop materially below the average, or two world-crops in succession not above the average in acre yield, shall be garnered.

Upon the assumption that the bread-eating populations will increase during the next thirty years at a rate only three-fourths that obtaining since 1871 ; recognising the indisputable fact that the United States have practically ceased to add materially to the acres bearing the great primary food staples; and remembering that since 1871 all the rest of the world has added less than 28,000,000 acres to these areas, it may be well to enquire where will be found the 200,000,000 fertile acres required to furnish the grain and potatoes needed by the 160,000,000 units which the suggested rate of increase—low as it is—will add to the consuming force within thirty years. We may afterwards enquire how provision is to be made for the existing deficit of more than 70,000,000 acres which then will be apparent whenever acre yields do not exceed the average of the last twenty-eight years.

In reply to an enquiry as to the dependence of the price of wheat on supply and demand, Mr Davis wrote last April in the following terms :—

It is true that conditions of supply and demand, so far as I can see, warrant higher prices for wheat, but so long as the market is dominated by phantom wheat ("futures") so long will the price remain low, unless actual scarcity is threatened in the immediate future. It will be four months before new winter wheat will reach American mills in any considerable measure, and five months before it can reach the European consumer. In the meantime the world must live upon the grain grown in 1898. Of the spring wheat (yet to be sown) of Minnesota, the Dakotas, and Manitoba not much can reach the mills until after the middle of September, and none reach the

European consumer until the middle of October, but unless a great calamity overtakes the fields of Europe or America the dealers will keep the price down by loading the markets with thousands of millions of bushels of "futures" that have the same effect upon prices as the offering of an equal amount of real wheat—provided scarcity is not threatened.

In 1892, when before a Congressional Committee, I was able to show from the reports of the New York Produce Exchange that in a single year 2,000,000,000 bushels of fictitious wheat (the equivalent of a world crop) had been sold upon that one market, and as much as 44,000,000 bushels in a single day (14th April 1890) although the sales of actual wheat on that day were but 6000 bushels, and but 18,000,000 bushels in the year! This phantom stuff—more nebulous than star dust—is sold by responsible parties, whose contracts are good for any amount of money; but the sales never mature into deliveries. They are either bought back, or are settled by payment of differences at maturity. In other words, these are simply gambling transactions that determine the price of wheat before the seed is sown—unless scarcity develops in the interim.

The gambling transactions of the professional dealer in "futures" are the least of the evils resulting from these detestable operations, as the "futures" system makes every miller or dealer who buys and sells it an enemy of real wheat. This is the anomaly which results in the other anomaly of low prices. The dealer and miller have from five to one hundred times as great an interest in phantom that he has in actual wheat, and therefore his influence in depressing the price is from five to one hundred times greater than his *possible* interest in advancing the price. For instance, the miller buys 10,000 bushels of wheat to-day to grind in his mill. Immediately it is bought he orders his broker to sell 10,000 bushels of July wheat in Chicago. That is wheat deliverable in July at Chicago. His mill grinds the wheat, say, in three days, and at the end of that time the flour is sold, but he has four months to watch the market and take in his contract at a lower price than he sold it for. At the end of the three days he has bought another 10,000 bushels of actual wheat to grind, sold another 10,000 bushels of actual in the form of flour, and put out another "futures" contract for a like 10,000 bushels. In this way, like Tennyson's brook, he goes on for ever, never taking in a contract before maturity unless he can buy it back at a profit. The result may be, and often is, that he is never interested in more than ten days' supply of actual wheat for his mill, while his "futures" are outstanding for as much wheat as he has ground in two, four, and even six months or more. That is, he is interested at all times in depressing the price on 250,000 bushels of wheat, but only interested in advancing it on a possible 20,000 bushels and often not on a single bushel, as he endeavours to contract for the sale of his flour before the actual wheat is bought from which it is to be made. This detestable "futures" system is the only one ever invented which makes the owner of actual property interested in destroying its price—and even in destroying the price of wheat which is yet to grow, as "futures" often run for a year. The dealer in actual grain sells his wheat to arrive, and sells "futures" against it the moment it is bought, so that actually there is no one but the hapless farmer with any interest whatever in advancing prices. What can the farmer do to advance prices with

the whole machinery of trade against him, unless scarcity
comes to his aid, as presumed scarcity did last spring,
when every dealer and miller aided in the advance, as
they will whenever wheat becomes scarce. And I *think*
the scarcity for the 1899-1900 harvest year is now
assured.

I think it is assured by conditions in the United States,
where the winter wheat crop has met with disaster, more
pronounced in Kansas than elsewhere. The State has
lost more than half its wheat outright, the remainder is
badly injured. We cannot grow more than a third as
much wheat in Kansas as in 1898, and I am of the opinion
that we shall not grow more than a fourth as much. In
this immediate vicinity not 20 per cent. of the wheat sown,
or area sown will be harvested, and most of this will,
probably, give but a meagre yield. Nebraska, Iowa,
a large part of Oklahoma, and most of Missouri, have
suffered nearly as badly as Kansas, while the State
report, issued a few days since by the Agricultural
officials in Tennessee, reports a loss of 30 per cent.
of the crop. In Illinois, Indiana, and Michigan the loss
is great, but much less than in Kansas, while serious
complaints come from New York, Pennsylvania, Maryland,
and Virginia. If there is a single state promising anything
approaching an average crop of winter wheat it is Ohio.
On the Pacific slope the promise is somewhat better, but
the injury in both Oregon and Washington is serious,
although this can and doubtless will be remedied in part
by resowing the devastated fields with spring wheat, as
may be done in Iowa and Nebraska to some extent.

Kansas will probably harvest 50,000,000 bushels less
than last year, and we lose all our own wheat but about
25 per cent., and that is in bad shape, and I shall be

surprised if our farm produces as much wheat as was sown last Fall.

The season in the spring wheat regions (Minnesota, the Dakotas, and Manitoba) is quite a month late now, and but little if any ploughing was done in the autumn, where usually from 60 to 75 per cent. on the ground intended for spring wheat is full ploughed. In these regions there is from 3 to 7 feet of frozen earth, and it will take weeks to thaw completely this stratum, and it will be impossible to plough until it is thawed, as the frozen earth below keeps the surface soil in a semi-liquid condition. Unless the season is unusually favourable, this promises to result in both a reduced area and yield of spring wheat per acre. Late sowing is almost always accompanied by a yield greatly lessened. From these conditions I look for a small wheat crop in the U.S. and greatly reduced exports, and from the fact that no winter wheat will be available—or but little winter wheat—for export, just after harvest Europe is likely to see comparative scarcity before its own product is available in October—that is available by the consumer. Long before October the wheat of India and Argentina will cease to trouble the market. This, however, all depends upon the correctness of my diagnosis of present and proximate conditions relating to the American crop.

AMERICA AND THE WHEAT PROBLEM*

BY JOHN HYDE

NOT since Tyndall shocked the religious sentiment of almost the entire English-speaking world by proposing, at the Belfast meeting in 1874, that certain wards of a hospital should be set apart for a scientific test of the efficacy of prayer, has the Annual Address of a President of the British Association for the Advancement of Science excited so general an interest, or provoked so much unfavourable criticism, as have the recent utterances of Sir William Crookes on the subject of an approaching scarcity in the supply of wheat. In the United States the warning—for such,

---

* This article was written for the *North American Review* for February last by the Hon. John Hyde, Statistician-in-Chief of the United States Department of Agriculture, probably the one man in America best qualified to deal with the subject. I am greatly indebted to the proprietors of the *North American Review* for permission to reprint this article, and to Mr Hyde for a supplementary note to his article, written specially for this volume.
160

rather than as a prediction, it should be considered —of the distinguished chemist has been received with a chorus of deprecation in which there was scarcely a discordant voice, the idea that the wheat-producing capabilities of this country are not practically illimitable being generally scouted as preposterous. Much of the criticism, however, was founded upon a telegraphic report, which, however creditable to newspaper enterprise, was not entirely accurate ; and now that the address is available in complete form, it may be worth our while to ex- amine it with some degree of care, with a view to determining its actual bearing upon prospective conditions in this country.

The field covered by Sir William's argument is of immense extent. It is practically the entire wheat-producing region of the world, and the potentiality of every considerable portion of it is discussed in more or less detail, and, in the main, conservatively. To follow the explorer, however, from Europe to Siberia, from Canada to Australia, from South America to Africa would be less useful, because less conclusive, than would be a considera- tion of the conditions, actual and prospective, in the United States, the country which, as he himself says, has for the last thirty years been the dominant factor in the world's supply. Sir William's refer-

L

ences to the United States constitute less than
one-twentieth part of his discussion of the wheat-
supply problem, and are mainly embodied in the
following statements :—

"Practically there remains no uncultivated prairie land
in the United States suitable for wheat growing. The
virgin land has been rapidly absorbed, until at present
there is no land left for wheat without reducing the area
for maize, hay, and other necessary crops.

"It is almost certain that within a generation the ever-
increasing population of the United States will consume all
the wheat grown within its borders, and will be driven to
import, and, like ourselves, will scramble for a lion's share
of the wheat crop of the world."

What it is sought to establish is, that not in
the immediate future, but when almost a third of
the coming century—practically a generation—shall
have passed away, the wheat supply of the world,
including the United States, will fall so far short of
the demand as to constitute general scarcity, unless
starvation be averted through the laboratory. This
is Sir William Crookes's contention, and it is the
object of the present article to consider, from a
standpoint somewhat different from that either of
the English chemist or his critics, what are likely
to be the prevailing agricultural conditions in the
United States a generation hence.

What were the conditions a generation ago? The country then had a population of about 34,000,000; now it has one of about 75,000,000, exclusive of the islands to be brought under its dominion as a result of the war with Spain. One hundred and ninety-one million bushels was the largest wheat crop on record; the average of the last three years has fallen but little, if any, short of 540,000,000 bushels. In the fiscal year 1865-66 the total exports of wheat, including wheat flour, were less than 16,500,000 bushels; last year they exceeded 217,000,000 bushels. In 1865 the maize crop was only 704,000,000 bushels, with 828,000,000 bushels as the high-water mark of previous production; during the last three years the crop has averaged over 2,000,000,000 bushels.

Were there really no limit to the agricultural potentiality of the United States, these enormous figures might furnish some sort of index to the probable developments of the future. But we are liable to be led seriously astray if we assume for the thirty-three years to come an increase proportionate to that of the thirty-three years last past. That the population of the United States in 1931, exclusive of colonial possessions or dependencies, will be at least 130,000,000 is as certain as any future event can be, but it is not nearly so easy

a matter to forecast the agricultural production of
that period; and yet the question that lies at the
very foundation of any just criticism of Sir William
Crookes's address is, what contribution, if any,
our farmers will be able to make to the wheat
supply of other countries, when the time comes
that provision has to be made for the varied
requirements of a home population more than
twice as large as that at the last federal census.

Those requirements will include a wheat crop of
700,000,000 bushels, without a bushel for export;
an oat crop of 1,250,000,000 bushels; a maize crop
of 3,450,000,000 bushels, and a hay crop of
100,000,000 tons, all for domestic consumption;
with cotton and wool, fruit and vegetables, dairy
and poultry products, meats and innumerable minor
commodities in corresponding proportions. The
area necessary to the production of the three
principal cereals alone will be over 15 per cent.
greater than the enormous total acreage devoted in
1898 to grain, cotton, and hay, while the mere
addition of the two last-mentioned products and of
the minor cereals will call for an acreage exceeding
the total area of improved land in farms at the
present time.

But what, it may be asked, is to prevent either
(1) any necessary extension of the areas in farms,

or (2) the bringing under cultivation of that large residue of unimproved land which amounted at the last federal census to no less than 42.6 per cent. of the total farm area?

The great fact that underlies the enormous productive capacity of the United States to-day is, of course, the transfer from government ownership to individual proprietors, within a single generation, of a body of land hundreds of millions of acres in extent, and for the most part of extraordinary fertility. But, amazing as has been the increase in the farm area of the country during the last thirty years, it has not been sufficient even to keep pace with the growth of population. The addition of 128,300,000 acres, or 31.48 per cent., to the area in farms between 1870 and 1880 only increased the area *per capita* of population from 10.57 to 10.69 acres. By 1890 the area, notwithstanding a further addition of 87,100,000 acres, or 16.25 per cent., amounted to only 9.95 acres *per capita*, and the census of 1900 will almost certainly find it under 9 acres.

That for general agricultural purposes the public domain is practically exhausted, and that, consequently, there can be no further considerable addition to the farm area of the country, is too well-established a fact to be the subject of controversy.

Of the entire area undisposed of, 72.7 per cent. is
in States wholly within the arid region, and all but
a small part of the remainder is desert, mountain,
or at best suitable only for grazing purposes.*   In
Kansas, out of 1,061,000 acres undisposed of, only
116,000 acres are east of the 100th meridian, and
these are described as broken and for the most part
sandy.   In Nebraska 10,548,000 acres are still open
to settlement, but not one acre in seven is in a
region of sufficient rainfall for general agricultural
purposes, and the best of the land is described by
the General Land Office as fit only for grazing.   In
North   Dakota   the   vacant   land   amounts   to
20,575,000 acres, but on little more than one-tenth
of this area could irrigation be dispensed with, even
if the land were otherwise adapted to general
farming.   In   Oklahoma,   the   youngest   of   the
territories, and the one containing the largest
addition to the farm area of the country that has
been made within many years, of the 7,007,000
acres of government land still vacant, 3,250,000

* The figures relative to the public lands, and the possibilities of
irrigation, are taken from the Report of the Secretary of the Interior
for the fiscal year ended 30th June 1898, pp. 15-16; the Annual
Reports of the Commissioner of the General Land Office for the fiscal
years ended 30th June 1897 and 1898, and The Public Lands and
their Water Supply, by Frederick Haynes Newell, Sixteenth Annual
Report of the U.S. Geological Survey, 1894-95, part ii., pp.
463-533.

acres lie between the 99th and 100th meridians, and a like amount, making altogether 93 per cent. of the whole, west of the 100th. The vacant land in the Pacific States amounts to 91,843,000 acres ; but of the 42,503,000 acres in California, 19,000,000 acres are "barren, irreclaimable wastes," 19,875,000 acres "desert and grazing," and 3,628,000 acres "woodland and forest"; the 35,898,000 acres in Oregon include 17,067,000 acres of "desert and grazing," and 18,831,000 acres of "woodland and forest," while the 13,443,000 acres in Washington comprise 3,847,000 acres of "desert and grazing," and 9,596,000 acres of "woodland and forest."

It should not be forgotten, in this connection, that it is no longer the policy of the American people, or of its representatives in Congress, to permit of the continued destruction of the national forests, without regard to the needs of the future. It should also be borne in mind that, according to the U.S. Geological Survey, the entire water supply of the Pacific States available for irrigation is only sufficient for some 23,000,000 additional acres, or about 1 acre in 4 of the unappropriated public lands in those states. In the entire arid region the available water supply, as similarly estimated by the U.S. Geological Survey, is only sufficient for the irrigation of 71,500,000 additional acres, or 1 acre in 7 and one-half of the area undisposed of. Commenting upon the difficulties encountered by the individual farmer in reclaiming land from its desert condition, the Commissioner of the General Land Office, in his Report for the fiscal year ended 30th June 1898, p. 72, calls attention to the fact that such reclamation amounts to " less than 125,000 acres annually, at which rate it would require nearly six hundred years to dispose of all the irrigable lands." Commissioner Hermann says further :—

"In connection with these astounding figures, it should not be overlooked that much the greater part of the lands already disposed of are those bordering on small streams, where reclamation was accomplished principally through individual efforts.

"Nearly all of the waters of these smaller streams are now utilised, and the remaining lands depend for their reclamation upon the saving of all overflow waters, and the diverting of the waters of the larger streams, which can be done only by expensive construction. It is, therefore, but a fair presumption that the disposal of desert lands to individuals will annually decrease, unless Congress, in its wisdom, provides a means by which the annual overflow waters in the arid region may be saved, and intelligently dispensed."

The extent to which the total farm area of the country can be increased by the reclamation of desert lands will therefore be seen to be very small, if not absolutely insignificant; indeed, it is a question whether it will be sufficient even to counterbalance those constant encroachments upon the productive area which arises from the growth of cities,* the building of railroads, and the general development of commerce and of non-agricultural industry.†

But what of that vast body of unimproved land already in farms, which amounted at the last census to 265,600,000 acres, or more than two-fifths of the total farm area of the country? Where is it situated, and of what does it consist?

If its distribution is not uniform with that of the area improved, it is no less general. No section of the country, large or small, has been too long settled, none has a too easily cultivable soil, none has too good a market in proximity to it, to be

* At the census of 1890, of the counties containing the twenty-eight most populous cities in the country, twenty had a smaller number of farms, and twenty-three a smaller farm area, and smaller area of improved land in farms, than they had in 1880. Of the exceptions, all but three were due to the increase in the number and area of market gardens, which, for census purposes, were considered as farms.

† It is difficult to estimate the amount of land annually withdrawn from the farm area of the country, but the statistics of improved and unimproved land at the Eleventh Census show incidentally that at least 4,500,000 acres of the former and 6,500,000 acres of the latter passed out of farms during the preceding ten years, an average of more than 1,000,000 acres per annum.

exempt from making a relatively substantial contribution to the unimproved acreage in farms.
There was not one of the 2783 counties at the
Eleventh Census that failed to contribute to the
grand total, whether situated in the richest part of
the Mississippi Valley, or embracing some great
centre of population.*

Between the international line and the 37th
parallel (which runs through Hampton Roads, Va.,
Cairo, Ill., across the southern part of Missouri,
and forms the northern boundary of Indian Territory
and Oklahoma) and east of the 100th meridian, the
census of 1890 found about 115,000,000 acres of
unimproved land in farms, ranging from 15.8 per
cent. of the total farm area in Illinois to 55.9 per
cent. of that in West Virginia. South of the 37th
parallel, and east of the 100th meridian there were
about 118,000,000 acres, ranging from 53.6 per
cent. of the total farm area in Tennessee to 68.8 per
cent. of that in Florida. Within the region that is
absolutely arid were about 27,000,000 acres, ranging from 53.4 per cent. of the total farm area in
Montana to 92 per cent. of that in Arizona, and in
those portions of the Pacific States in which

---

* The counties containing the cities of New York, Boston, Jersey
City, St Louis, and San Francisco, had 115, 451, 135, 422, and 366 acres
of unimproved land in farms, respectively.

irrigation is unnecessary were found the remaining 5,500,000 acres.

The chief factor in determining the ratio of unimproved land in farms to total farm area is not the cost of the land, not the facility with which it has been acquired, but the relative facility of cultivation. The percentage of unimproved land is higher in all the New England States, except Connecticut, than in either of the two Dakotas, with their immense areas of newly opened farms, and it is higher in almost every southern State than even in Montana, Idaho, Utah, or Nevada.

The enumerators of the Tenth and Eleventh Censuses were instructed to report as "improved" all tilled land, including fallow and grass in rotation, whether pasture or meadow, and all permanent meadows, permanent pastures, orchards and vineyards. As "unimproved" they were instructed to report all natural woodland and forest within farm limits, all unploughed land, and all land that, once ploughed, has since been abandoned for cultivation, like the "old fields" of the South. They were specifically directed that rocky, hill and mountain pastures were not to be reported as improved land.

With this distinction clearly in mind, a brief survey of the conditions existing in the grand divisions above specified should prove instructive.

With regard, first, to the unimproved land in
farms in the arid region, there will apply with
almost equal force much of what has been quoted
from the Report of the Commissioner of the General
Land Office against the probability of any considerable increase in the total farm area.   On irrigated
lands, the yield per acre is relatively so high that
the farmer in the arid region has every inducement
to utilise, to the fullest extent, such portions of his
farm as are irrigable.   The land easily irrigated has,
therefore, to a large extent, been already brought
under cultivation, and is annually contributing to the
fruit, grain, and forage crops of the country.   The
developments of the future will be slow and costly.
The average first cost of preparing the soil for
cultivation in the arid region, as determined by
Mr Frederick H. Newell, in connection with the
Eleventh Census,* was $13.51 per acre, and the
average first cost of water rights $8.23 per acre,
making $21.74 as the average cost per acre of
reclaiming such of the desert lands as were the
most easily irrigated.   In the eight States and
territories lying wholly within the arid region, the
irrigated land   constituted   but   little   more   than

* Report on Agriculture by Irrigation in the Western part of the
United States at the Eleventh Census, 1890.   By F. H. Newell,
Special Agent.   1894.

two-fifths of the land reported as in some sense improved, so the chances for the reclamation of the still larger body of land, upon which no improvements whatever had been made, are exceedingly remote. They are, for the most part, grazing lands, and such they will doubtless remain.

Among the various astounding assertions called forth by the discussion of Sir William Crookes's address is the statement that, with wheat at a dollar per bushel, the annual production of that cereal in the state of Idaho alone might reach 400,000,000 bushels! It is amazing that such an assertion should be given place in an article written in 1898 for a scientific publication. While farming without irrigation is successful along the north-western edge of this most interesting and beautiful State, the State is, for the most part, made up of mountain, forest, and desert. Its mean elevation is 4,700 feet, and over 15,000 square miles of its area is from 6,000 to 11,000 feet above sea-level. Many of its valleys and the lower slopes of its mountains are covered with a dense forest, the removal of which would be only preparatory to the construction of more or less costly irrigation works. Of every 100 acres of its land surface, statistically considered, 84 acres are still without settlers, and of these 34 acres are desert and 50

acres forest. The entire arable land of the State
has been estimated by Mr Henry Gannett,
geographer of the U.S. Geological Survey, and of
the Tenth and Eleventh Censuses, at rather less
than 4,000,000 acres, and Mr F. H. Newell, hydro-
grapher of the U.S. Geological Survey, in estimating the water-supply as sufficient for the reclamation of 7,000,000 acres, makes, by implication, the
highest estimate of the agricultural possibilities of
the State that has been made by any competent and
disinterested authority. Even the State Engineer
estimates the amount of land that can ultimately
be cultivated by irrigation in Idaho as not more
than 4,000,000 or 5,000,000 of acres in the
aggregate.* On the basis of reports from nearly
500 local correspondents, the Department of
Agriculture estimates the wheat crop of Idaho for
the present year at but little more than 4,000,000
bushels, while commercial authorities in general
content themselves with including it, with other
States of small production, under the head of
"other" or "sundry." What a fortunate thing it is
that the country has been warned in advance, so that
business may not be too seriously demoralised by
the sudden marketing of a 400,000,000 bushel crop!

* First Biennial Report of the State Engineer to the Governor of
Idaho, December 1896, p. 7.

Let us turn now to that important group of States lying south of the 37th parallel, and wholly or mainly east of the 100th meridian. These States contain about 22 per cent. of the entire land surface of the country, and about 29 per cent. of its total farm area. But, while their improved farm acreage is only 21 per cent. of that of the country at large, the land included in their farms and plantations, and remaining in a state of nature, constitutes no less than 44 per cent. of the total unimproved farm area of the country, or a larger proportion of the total farm area within which it is embraced than is to be found in any other group of States, not excepting even those of the arid region. The reason for this is not far to seek. Excluding Texas, the unimproved land, of which is mainly prairie, of every 100 acres of unimproved land in farms in the States under con-sideration 89 were at the Tenth Census covered with forest and woodlands, the percentage ranging from 78 in South Carolina to 93 in Florida and Arkansas.

The soil of this forest area* is to a large extent

* See Report on Cotton Production in the United States, by E. W. Hilgard, Ph.D., vols. v.-vi. of the Tenth Census Reports. Forestry Conditions and Interests of Wisconsin, by Filibert Roth, U.S. Depart-ment of Agriculture, 1898, may also be consulted with reference to the use of pine-lands for agricultural purposes.

of so inferior a quality that there is but little inducement to attempt its reclamation, and, even after the
merchantable timber has been removed from it, but
little effort is made to utilise it for farm purposes.
This is owing to the fact that it is its mechanical
rather than its chemical constitution that presents
the most serious obstacle to such utilisation. Containing, for the most part, an exceedingly large
percentage of sand, the obstacle it presents to
successful cultivation is not one that can be over-
come by the use of commercial fertilisers, except
for forage crops and vegetables.

While, therefore, each succeeding census will
probably find some relatively small portion of it
added to the cultivated lands of the various States,
it cannot have the slightest bearing upon the much
discussed wheat problem. For such wheat production as the farmers of the South are engaged
in, the lands best adapted to the growth of that
cereal are assigned, and yet, in the ten years ending
with 1897, the ten principal cotton States produced
an average annual crop of only 23,610,671 bushels,
the average annual yield per acre being only 8
bushels. Between 1880 and 1890 these States,
together with Virginia, increased their area in
cotton by 5,630,000 acres, their area in maize by
1,140,000 acres, their area mown by 1,320,000 acres,

and the number of their milch cows by 630,000. Their area in wheat, however, showed a decline of 1,150,000 acres, a fact that need occasion no surprise when it is considered that the average value of farm products per acre of improved land in these States is in inverse ratio to the extent of their wheat production.

There are writers who seem to imagine that the price or exchangeability of a product is the sole factor in determining the extent of its production everywhere and at all times ; but this certainly does not hold good where the cultivation of the product is so difficult and precarious as is that of wheat in the southern States. For this reason, were wheat to be worth a dollar per bushel, no largely increased production need be looked for in the South. From 1879 to 1883, inclusive, the average price of wheat in Chicago was $1.08, and even the average December farm price was $1.01. During these five years, however, the total wheat production of the ten principal cotton States averaged only 24,270,000, bushels per annum, or about 660,000 bushels more than the average during the ten years ending with 1897. It is not, of course, contended that $1 per bushel fifteen or twenty years ago was the equivalent of the same price at the present time, but simply that a relatively high price failed to

M

increase production, owing to the limitations imposed by physical conditions.

In discussing agricultural potentialities, much
misconception arises from taking the state as the
geographical unit. From the fact that North
Carolina contributes annually some 4,000,000 or
5,000,000 bushels of wheat to the total production
of the country, it might be supposed that its production could be very largely increased; but an
examination of the statistics by counties discloses
the fact that the crop is grown almost entirely on
the high lands on the western border of the State,
adjoining the Blue Ridge and Great Smoky
Mountains; and with regard to the adjoining State
of South Carolina, no less than 97 per cent. of its
wheat crop at the last census was produced in the
counties embraced within the Piedmont and Alpine
sections of the State. Still, the average annual
yield per acre in the two States for the last ten
years has been only 6.3 and 5.9 bushels respectively.

In Tennessee, Texas, and Oklahoma,. the conditions are somewhat different from those obtaining
in the other States south of the 37th parallel, but
the favourable conditions that render possible the
larger production in these States are more or less
localised, and no really great extension of this
branch of agriculture is to be looked for within their

borders, even under the stimulus of high prices. This is equally true of Indian Territory, a region that lies wholly within the Lower Austral life zone, and the large and increasing cotton production of which is itself the very strongest argument against the possibility of developments in the production of wheat that will be more than a mere drop in the bucket. Nature has decreed that a profitable return on the cost of cultivation shall become less and less to be depended on the farther the departure from the region to which the plant is indigenous, and the operation of this law can be arrested, in the case of wheat growing, only by topographic conditions— chiefly that of elevation above sea-level—that do not exist in Indian Territory.*

It is the firm belief of the writer that with a more diversified agriculture—in the direction of which a gratifying tendency is already observable. —and with the continued development of its manufacturing industries, the South will soon enter upon an era of great prosperity, but its contribution to the wheat crop will continue to be but small.

This brings us to the consideration of that

* The Republic of Mexico had a very creditable exhibit of wheat at the recent Trans-Mississippi Exposition at Omaha, but it was grown at an elevation of several thousand feet above sea-level.

marvellous agricultural region extending from the international line to the 37th parallel, and from the Atlantic Ocean to the 100th meridian—a region containing only 30 per cent. of the entire land surface of the country, but yet embracing 59 per cent. of its total farm area, and nearly 71 per cent. of its improved farm acreage. The twenty-six States in this division contributed last year 82 per cent. of the total maize crop, 76 per cent. of the total wheat crop, 91 per cent. of the total oat crop, 83 per cent. of the total hay crop, and a correspondingly large proportion of the total production of every other agricultural product, save cotton, sugar cane, and the tropical and sub-tropical fruits grown in the United States. It is obvious, moreover, that this is the region that must continue to furnish the principal proportion of all these necessary commodities.

The fact that at the census of 1890 these States contained about 115,000,000 acres of unimproved land in farms would suggest enormous agricultural possibilities, but unfortunately these large figures are to some extent delusive. Here, as in other parts of the country, the distribution of the unimproved land is anything but uniform, and the extent to which such land might be made available for cultivation likewise differs widely.

In Illinois and Iowa it constitutes between 15 and 20 per cent. of the total farm area; in New York, New Jersey, Pennsylvania, Delaware, Ohio, Indiana, Kansas, and Nebraska between 20 and 30 per cent.; in Vermont, Connecticut, Maryland, Michigan, Missouri, North Dakota, and South Dakota between 30 and 40 per cent.; in Massachusetts, Rhode Island, Kentucky, Wisconsin, and Minnesota between 40 and 50 per cent.; and in Maine, New Hampshire, Virginia, and West Virginia, between 50 and 60 per cent. It will readily occur to the reader that these differences are largely a matter of topography—indeed, only a superficial acquaintance with the natural characteristics of the different States is necessary to placing nearly all of them in their respective categories. The question is: How near do these various figures come to indicating the amount of additional land that might be brought under cultivation under the stimulus of higher prices for agricultural products? This we should be able to determine with a sufficiently close approximation to the truth by a brief examination of the conditions obtaining in certain typical States.

Beginning with Illinois, we find that at the Eleventh Census that State contained 10,116 miles of railroad and 69 towns and cities of 3,000 inhabitants or upward, of which 21 contained 10,000 or upward. It had enjoyed periods of great agricultural prosperity since it became fully settled ; it possessed within its borders the greatest produce market and shipping point in the world; its agriculture was of the most diversified character, and its farmers had every inducement to make the most of the agricultural capabilities of their farms. Is it unreasonable, then, to suppose that its residue of unimproved land, 15.8 per cent., represented, if not an absolutely irreducible minimum, at least that proportion of the entire farm area which—containing, as it did, not only all waste land, but farm-yards, private roads, wood lots, and natural pastures—not even an era of high prices would bring under cultivation? In Iowa the conditions were in all essential respects the same, and the percentage of unimproved land differed but very slightly, being 16.6 per cent. of the whole. Ohio has been longer settled, but its surface is more broken, and its percentage was 21.5. In Pennsylvania the percentage was 28.1, many counties in the mountain region averaging over 40 per cent., and some very much higher. In Kentucky a naturally somewhat high percentage is rendered still higher by the inclusion of many fine natural parks and pastures among the unimproved. In Kansas, Nebraska, Minnesota, and the Dakotas, averages of from 26 to 40 per cent. are mainly attributable to the more recent settlement of those States.

Assuming that the entire region will, under the influence of high prices, have 85 per cent. of its total farm area brought under cultivation within the next thirty years, there will be added to the productive area in this region about 60,000,000 acres, with State and railroad lands to the possible extent of 20,000,000 acres in addition. This will fall so far short of the requirements of our own population that it is necessary to seek other possible additions to the cultivable area.

Not for the purpose of growing wheat, but under the influence of those generally higher prices which any considerable and long-continued increase in the price of wheat would bring about by reducing the acreage in other products, the South might conceivably add to her productive area as much as 30,000,000 acres. Ten million acres might be added on the Pacific coast and 3,000,000 acres in the arid region. This would make the gross addition 123,000,000 acres, against which must be set those continual withdrawals of land from agricultural uses which not even a high degree of agricultural prosperity would entirely prevent.

Assuming the annual rate of diversion to be diminished by one-half, the loss during the next thirty years would amount to about 15,000,000 acres, making the net increase 108,000,000 acres.

This will constitute an enormous addition to the productive capacity of the farms of the country, and one, the contemplation of which, aside from the question of consumption, might well appal our much-discouraged farmers. Considered, however, in the light of the requirements of a population of 130,000,000, the figures assume an entirely different aspect. On the basis of our present actual consumption as a people, to the entire exclusion of our export trade, the country will require by the year 1931 the following additional acreage—for wheat, 13,500,000 acres; for maize, 66,000,000 acres; for oats, 23,700,000 acres; for the minor cereals, 10,000,000 acres, and for hay, 40,500,000 acres, a total of 153,700,000 acres, without making any provision for the proportionately increased consumption of vegetables, fruits, and other products. Instead, therefore, of the probably largely increased acreage bringing down prices, or proving unprofitable to the farmers, there will be a deficiency of at least 50,000,000 acres. Indeed, it will be more than this, since it cannot be supposed for a moment that the unimproved lands left to the last are anything like equal in natural fertility to those first selected for cultivation. On the other side of the account, however, we have to place whatever increase in yield per acre may be brought about by improved methods of farming. But whatever agricultural science may be able to do in this direction within the next thirty years, up to the present time it has only succeeded in arresting that decline in the rate of production with which we have been continually threatened.

From 1878 to 1882, inclusive, the average yield per acre of wheat was 12.8 bushels; from 1883 to 1887 it was 11.9 bushels; from 1888 to 1892 it was 12.8 bushels, and from 1893 to 1897 it was likewise 12.8 bushels. While it has been remarkably uniform when considered in five-year periods, it would unquestionably show a slight decline were it not for the very high averages obtaining in those States and territories the crops of which are irrigated, and which have appeared in the list of wheat-growing States only within the last fifteen years. The average yield per acre of maize for the ten-year period 1878-87 was 24.40 bushels; from 1888 to 1897 it was 24.42 bushels. Of oats the average yield was 27.2 bushels in the former and 25.7 bushels in the latter period. Of potatoes the average yield per acre declined from 77.6 bushels to 76.0 bushels; of cotton it declined from 181 lbs. to 172 lbs. and of tobacco from 727 lbs to 726 lbs. Of hay the latter period shows an increase of one-hundredth of a ton per acre per annum, and there is also a slight increase in the case of barley, rye, and buckwheat.

While there is but little satisfaction to be obtained from these figures, it must be borne in mind that it is only to a very small extent indeed that scientific methods have as yet been employed in the growing of field crops. It is unquestionably to the laboratory that we shall have to look for relief, except in so far as it may be afforded by the Government undertaking the construction of storage reservoirs in the arid region that might reclaim, not to exceed 71,500,000 acres, less whatever small area might in the meantime have been brought under cultivation in that region through private enterprise.

So much as to the prospective crop situation in general; what as to the question of wheat production? That it is to the crop most readily convertible into money that, all other things being equal, the farmer will give the preference in determining what he will grow, needs no proof. The cultivation of wheat at the expense of other necessary crops will, however, be held in check by two very powerful influences. The first will arise from the fact that a reduction of the acreage under any product of general use below the actual requirements of the country will instantly—perhaps even prospectively—affect the price of that product, possibly in a proportion even greater than that by which its acreage is diminished, and may even be sufficient to constitute it a competitor with wheat on equal terms for the farmer's favour. The second check will be found in the fact that the American farmer, north, south, east, and west, has at last fully awakened to the safety, stability, and, in the long run, increased profit resulting from a judiciously diversified system of farming. The one-crop system has passed away, never to return, and before wheat can be extensively cultivated at the expense of other products it will not only have to command what would now appear to us an excessively high price, and afford a reasonable assurance of its continuing so to do, but would have to do this without affecting to any considerable extent the price of other products.

There is yet one more factor to be considered, namely, the possibility that, to a much larger extent than has ever yet been attempted or contemplated, the farmers in the different sections of the country will restrict their products to what they can raise most abundantly and most cheaply, so that the regions best adapted to wheat shall raise wheat, and so on through the entire category of farm products. This, however, would also be to a very large extent counter to that system of diversification which the writer regards as the most encouraging feature of the agriculture of our time, and while some change may be looked for in this direction, it is doubtful if it will play any very important part in our new rural economy.

To discuss the extent to which under conceivable conditions the United States may, notwithstanding this somewhat dubious outlook, still continue to contribute to the food supply of other nations, would be little more than speculation. It is sufficient for the writer's present purpose to have called attention to the enormous prospective increase in the requirements of our own population, and to some of the changes in the agricultural situation which such increase will involve.

APPENDIX

THERE is nothing in Mr Atkinson's second article (*Pop. Sc. Monthly*, April 1899) to which I should think it necessary to reply, were his English readers in possession of those facilities for testing the accuracy of his statements which are within the reach of his own countrymen. Several of his statements, however, possess all that extreme plausibility with which he is capable of investing even the most erroneous assertions, while some of his most confident assumptions and innocent-looking implications are, if possible, more dangerous than his direct statements.

Disdaining to study the intricate and difficult problem under consideration, in its relation to those highly diversified conditions of soil and climate necessarily obtaining in a region extending from the sub-arctic to the sub-tropic, and profoundly modified by a unique topography, Mr Atkinson coolly assumes that out of 3,000,000 square miles, 2,000,000 are arable ! An allowance of 1,000,000 square miles for land unavailable for agricultural purposes may, by reason of its very magnitude, strike the reader as liberal, as it was doubtless intended it should do, but what are the facts? What percentage of the total land surface is under cultivation in those States, the soil of which lends itself most readily to tillage, and in which agriculture has attained its fullest development? Illinois and Iowa are the two greatest agricultural States in the Union. A larger proportion of their area is cultivable, and a larger proportion actually cultivated, than of that of any equally extensive area in the world. At the last census they contained 442,584 farms, valued at £441,760,000; their live stock included 2,600,000 farm horses, 8,000,000 cattle, and 14,000,000 swine; and among the manifold products of their soil were 932,000,000 bushels of maize, wheat, and oats. The traveller journeying across their broad expanse by any one of half-a-dozen lines of railway looks out, from sunrise to sunset, on a region that, except for the occurrence of thriving manufacturing towns at more or less frequent intervals, might almost be taken for one vast farm. In consequence of the encroachments referred to in my former article,* Illinois has already attained and begun to recede from, while Iowa is rapidly approaching, the extreme limit, extensionally,

* Page 169.

of its agricultural development, and in both States the farmer has had every possible inducement to make the most of the capabilities of his farm. Nevertheless, in neither Illinois nor Iowa has more than 71.6 per cent. of the land surface ever been cultivated, and yet, of the entire country, with its 1,350,000 square miles of arid, and 250,000 square miles of semi-arid or sub-humid land, its Appalachian and minor mountain systems, and its various other topographic features and physical conditions unfavourable to agriculture, and absolutely unknown in Illinois and Iowa, Mr Atkinson would have us believe that 66.6 per cent. is arable and available !

Another statement to which strong exception must be taken is, that inasmuch as the wheat production of Dakota increased from less than 3,000,000 bushels in 1879 to about 100,000,000 bushels in 1898, Montana and Idaho, the annual production of which has never yet reached 6,500,000 bushels, may in time become correspondingly large producers. While it is quite possible that in his next article Mr Atkinson may plead that he did not mean to say Montana and Idaho, and may again blame the type-writing machine for his own mistake, I can only take his statement as he made it, and answer that there is absolutely no analogy, so far as concerns this discussion, between the condition of Dakota in 1879 and that of Montana and Idaho in 1898. In 1879 the immense agricultural potentiality of Dakota was widely recognised. The fact was perfectly well known that the territory contained millions of acres of exceedingly rich land, almost as level as a table, favoured, for the most part, with an abundant rainfall, and awaiting only that influx of population which must inevitably attend the throwing open of the land to settlement, and the impending extension of the territory's then utterly inadequate railway system. Montana and Idaho, on the other hand, are among the most mountainous States in the Union, are entirely within the arid region, and, with the exception of the north-western corner of Idaho, contain only a few strips of ground, on the low-lying and naturally irrigated banks of some of their streams, where agriculture is not absolutely dependent on the artificial application of water, a commodity—for such it is—of which there is not sufficient to irrigate 1 acre in 6. Moreover, while Dakota, in 1879, had a total of only 257 miles of railway, Montana and Idaho, in 1898, had 4010 miles, affording the most ample facilities either for taking settlers in or bringing produce out.

Never are Mr Atkinson's peculiar methods of conducting an argument more open to criticism than when he condescends to the use of authorities.

While his latest article is professedly based to a very large extent upon the testimony of the best informed men in the different States, he fails to quote the particular authority relied upon in so much as a single instance. Candid enough to acknowledge that he received only twenty-four detailed replies from the hundred persons appealed to, he yet manifestly seeks to create the impression that his entire argument is buttressed by the collective testimony of " the men who know the subject." He does not even give the names, nor yet the States, of the twenty-four persons who took the trouble to comply with his request, although he has no difficulty in finding room for an expression of his opinions on the tariff question, and even for some characteristic abuse of that overwhelming majority of his countrymen who refuse to shirk the responsibilities devolving upon them in connection with our new territorial possessions. How many of the twenty-four belonged to " the body of well-trained men in charge of the Agricultural Experiment Stations " he is most careful not to tell us, but he refers to these gentlemen, and to the excellence of their work, so frequently, and emphasises so strongly the value and importance of their opinions, that it is clearly his intention to create the impression that they constituted his main reliance. Now, notwithstanding the fact that not half a dozen of them may in any way share in Mr Atkinson's responsibility, it is proper to state, in view of the prominence given to them collectively, that however excellent their work—and much of it is excellent—it is not of a character to constitute them competent witnesses in the discussion of the question at issue. Their work is purely experimental, and along lines that, with few and unimportant exceptions, are as far removed from the question of the wheat-producing potentiality of their respective States as they well can be.

It would be interesting to know the authority, other than Mr Atkinson himself, for the statements that of the 56,000 square miles in Illinois, and the 68,000 square miles in Missouri, 54,000 and 64,000 respectively are arable. If " arable " means anything whatever in this connection, it must carry with it the idea of availability for agricultural uses, and yet the total farm area in Illinois at the last census, already *in process of reduction* through the encroachments of the non-agricultural industries, the growth of cities, and the construction of railways, was only 47,653 square miles, and that in Missouri 48,094 square miles! Although it should scarcely be necessary to demonstrate the recklessness of Mr Atkinson's statements, after his wonderful story of the natural deposits of phosphate of potash, the fact that he has not simply made a few excusable errors, but that his entire article is full of misstatements and unwarrantable assumptions, cannot be made too clear.

But what if the typical statements I have criticised were true, what bearing would the fact have on the wheat problem? Mr Atkinson evidently expects the reader to say to himself: "Two million square miles arable! 1,280,000,000 acres arable! Who, after this, can doubt that the wheat-producing potentiality of the United States is, as Mr Atkinson claims, immeasurable?" But, supposing that of the whole of this vast country, extending from the latitude of northern France to that of central Sahara, and with an infinite diversity of physical conditions, two-thirds were actually arable, would that necessarily mean a large increase in the production of wheat? Why is it that 400 counties, representing 15 per cent. of the entire area of the country, do not raise a single bushel of wheat, and that the sporadic production of 300 others, representing nearly 12 per cent. of the total area, aggregates only about one peck of wheat to each square mile? Why is it that the small section of the State of Arkansas lying north of 35° 45′ produces 83 per cent. of the wheat grown in the State but only 8 per cent. of the cotton? Why is it that there are extensive and prosperous agricultural communities that do not know what growing wheat looks like?

The only consideration of the wheat problem in the United States that has any claim whatever upon public confidence is one that starts with the fullest recognition of those wide differences of soil and climate which are found, in not a few cases, even within the limits of a single State, and yet this is just the consideration that Mr Atkinson is apparently unwilling to give it.

JOHN HYDE.

INDEX

INDEX